TALES FROM THE
KURTHERIAN UNIVERSE

TALES FROM THE KURTHERIAN UNIVERSE

BOOK THREE

MICHAEL ANDERLE   SAMANTHA HARMER
T.L. GRYFEN   KAT N. SNOW   LUCINDA PEBRE
LOGAN CAIRD   DOMINIC NOVIELLI   LISA FRETT
S.E. WEIR

DISRUPTIVE IMAGINATION

LMBPN Publishing
PMB 196, 2540 South Maryland Pkwy
Las Vegas, NV 89109

First US edition, September 2018
Version 1.01, September 2018

TALES FROM THE KURTHERIAN UNIVERSE
BOOK 3 TEAM

Thanks to the JIT Readers

John Ashmore
Mary Morris
Daniel Weigert
Erika Everest
James Caplan
Tim Bischoff
Kelly O'Donnell
Tracey Byrnes
Larry Omans
Micky Cocker

If I've missed anyone, please let me know!

Editor
Lynne Stiegler

Stories. Just about every human being loves them. Whether you absorb stories from books, magazines, the Internet, tv, movies, or you leaning over your mom or dad as they tell you something they did when they were young, pleasure is derived from listening to a good story.

And telling one (or two or three…a bunch.)

Until Amazon democratized the publishing business, we usually had to go through other people to get our stories read by others. Then, if an agent read our story, they had to like it enough to represent us and push our book on editors at the various publishing houses.

When I published my first set of stories, the desire to see my stories sell was a huge bucket list item (you know, that list of 'things to do before I die?') When I conceived the idea for Fans Write for the Fans, it was partially to give some of my fans the chance to go through the process of writing and then seeing their name in print.

They would get to see THEIR names on Amazon, and

become published and paid authors. But I didn't realize it would become so much more.

Authors in our Fans Write series have found friends around the world, and in their own backyards. Working together, supporting each other (In the Fans Write Facebook group) members have written stories, helped others with their stories, and frankly, some have had their lives changed.

The many good things happening went beyond my simple thoughts, and although I started the project, I'm not the one responsible for the amazing community it is now. The credit goes to Erika, Sarah and Nat—the ladies who took the opportunity I gave and watered it, allowing many others to share with book 02 and now book 03 of Fans Write for Fans.

To all of you who helped the authors in this book with your support, encouragement, beta reading, editing, and JIT reading, thank you! You have played an important role in the creation of this book.

To those authors whose stories are in this book, congratulations! Originally, the Fans Write project was to be a collection of fan fiction. However, through Lynne and others the requirement to honor canon became a thing, and now you have accomplished something rather remarkable.

You have been selected out of many submissions to be published with a story judged by our readers to honor the canon of The Kurtherian Gambit. Your name will be listed on the front, and you will be able to say for the rest of your life that you are a published author.

When I realized I was officially an author (that name on the cover thing), it was a damned good feeling.

I hope you enjoy the feeling like I did (and still do)!

Ad Aeternitatem,

Michael Anderle

HAIKU FROM THE KURTHERIAN UNIVERSE

Implacable death
pursues Kurtherian foes.
BA is coming...

Look for more throughout the book :)

A CONCERT TO REMEMBER

BY SAMANTHA HARMER

The Leath War has taken its toll. Three schoolgirls affected by loss attempt to bring solace to those left behind with a celebration to remember. For one night only, Jemma, Eleanor, and Mel present - The Mamas and the Ta-Tas!

But will anyone notice?

For all those in Fans Write who encouraged me to write this story. You know who you are.
— Samantha

A CONCERT TO REMEMBER

QBBS *Meredith Reynolds*, **High School**

Jemma glanced at the clock. The day had gone slowly, as it always did on a school day. *At least today is Friday, so I'll have two days of rest and relaxation.* She didn't hate school, she just wanted to do more. In three years her class would graduate and have a role in the Empire, but Jemma couldn't wait that long.

Last Career Day, the school organized a visit from some of the students' idols. Scientists, engineers, Marines, and others enticed them with placements. These offers came with a proviso—work hard at school. Very few of the girls wanted to join the Marines, but hell, they attended just to drool over the hunks in their oh-so-tight uniforms. Jemma smiled at the memory, wishing one of them was teaching their class right now.

At fifteen years old, Jemma wished she could do something that mattered. *Hell, I'll never be a fighter, but there must be other ways I can help. All I've ever wanted is to help people.* The idea of violence left a bitter taste in Jemma's mouth. A lump formed in her throat, and she coughed. Last year she had decided to be a doctor but discovered blood and needles made her faint. Jemma's heart broke at the thought of people suffering. That would be a start.

Jemma looked around the room, hoping for any distraction to relieve the boredom of Mr. Jameson's math class. His voice droned on, and she had to stifle a yawn. With sadness, she noticed the many empty chairs. She thought about her friend Melanie and the others attending the memorial services for their loved ones who had given their lives in the Leath war.

The passage of time hadn't improved the situation. Loss was loss. The community came together to honor the dead, and to help the living rebuild their lives.

This evening she and Eleanor had to cheer up their girl. Melanie had lost her mother in the last assault and had been living in a waking nightmare since then. They had all been prepared for the loss, but it hadn't helped.

For tonight, Jemma and Eleanor had found a collection of the old music, films, and games that Melanie liked. They'd also packed their overnight bags and arranged with Mel's father Robert to stay over at their apartment. They planned to shower her with girliness—anything to crack a smile.

Jemma watched the clock's hands crawl slowly toward two. One more hour and they'd be free.

QBBS *Meredith Reynolds*, Mel's Quarters

Robert opened the door, "Hi, girls, come inside. Mel's

just getting changed." He pointed toward Mel's door with a sad smile.

"How are you, Robert?" Jemma was worried about him. She'd known the Collins family for ten years, and they were like her extended family. His face was pale, and he looked tired and more careworn than she had ever seen him. Without thinking, she gave him a hug, willing as much healing into it as she could.

"I've been better, Jem. Mel's so quiet, I can't..." He stopped and swallowed audibly. "I can't get through to her. Her mother always knew the right words, I... I don't know where to begin." He fell quiet and stepped back from the hug, "Thank you. I'll get dinner ready. No doubt you girls are hungry."

They nodded to him and watched in silent sadness as a once-strong man made his way into the kitchen area. Jemma and Eleanor looked at each other.

Eleanor glanced at the closed door, "Are we planning to wait out here for Mel?"

"No. Let's face it, Mel will hide in her room all night if we let her. We're meant to be giving her company." So saying, Jemma walked to the door and knocked.

Melanie didn't respond, so Jemma raised her voice. "Mel, it's Jemma. Eleanor and I thought you could use our company tonight. Can we talk?"

No noise came from Melanie's room. After an awkward pause, the door slowly opened, revealing a small, slim girl with blond hair and eyes red from crying. Her blotchy face and red nose hid her natural beauty. With a nod of her head, she indicated that they should enter.

Jemma stopped short when she saw the room. Melanie

liked her room tidy; she'd always been a neat freak. It was like a tornado had hit it. Jemma paused, her mind racing for what to say. Tissues littered the bed and bedside table, clothes were strewn over the floor and books lay neglected everywhere.

Melanie noticed her reaction and looked around the room. Slowly her face changed from an expression of sadness to one of grim determination. Grumbling under her breath, she began to tidy her room.

"Well, Mel, I never thought I'd live to see the day when *my* room is cleaner than yours," Jemma began before she had time to stop herself. She looked guiltily at her friend. "Sorry, hon."

"No, you're right." Mel half-smiled. "I've let this place go to hell. If Mom were here, she'd yell at me. Tell me to pull myself together and take pride in my room."

"We brought music." Eleanor spoke up for the first time since entering the room. "Maybe it will help the chores go faster."

Brandishing an old mp3 player and speakers, Eleanor pressed Play. The girls started to clean up, occasionally sharing memories about things in the room.

As Mel replaced the last book on the shelf, their favorite song started playing. Eleanor, usually so quiet, sang along, and Jemma and Mel played backup. They danced around the room acting out the lyrics, hands raising to indicate their ring finger whenever the song mentioned it.

They got to the end and collapsed on the bed, laughing and tired. Enthusiastic applause interrupted the next track, and the girls leapt to their feet, eyes wide and cheeks flushed.

A smile lit Robert's face. "That was amazing. You girls have talent."

They beamed at him. Jemma noticed he looked younger than when he'd opened the door to them, as if a weight had been lifted from his shoulders.

"Mom loved that song," Mel said quietly. "She used to sing it all the time."

"Yes, she did." Robert motioned to his daughter to come over for a hug. "She would have loved to see you enjoying it as much as she did."

Mel ran to her father's arms and buried herself in his chest, tiny sobs escaping. Robert stroked her hair. Over Mel's head, he mouthed to Jemma and Eleanor, "Thank you."

Inside, Jemma felt proud that she'd helped.

"Well, girls, I hope you are hungry, because I may have cooked too much food." Robert laughed warmly.

They followed him out of the room to enjoy the feast.

QBBS *Meredith Reynolds*, High School Cafeteria, Monday

Mel slammed her tray down and looked disgusted. "You know, guys are idiots."

Eleanor threw a worried glance at Jemma. They knew Mel liked a boy called Owen, but he didn't notice her attempts to flirt with him.

"What's Owen done this time?" Jemma asked wearily.

Mel shot her an annoyed glance. "He's basically saying he's thinking of going to the end-of-year dance alone. Do you know why?" Her voice became heated.

Jemma shook her head, knowing it would be something stupid.

"Because he doesn't think anyone would want to go with him!" she growled through gritted teeth.

Jemma wanted to yell at her but instead asked, "Why don't you just ask him?"

Mel's glare was acid. "That would be so uncool. Plus, I'm not sure I'm going either." She relaxed a little. "I'm not in a party mood. Don't get me wrong; I loved that you two came to cheer me up the other night. I just don't want the rest of the school judging me for mourning. I mean, it's in two weeks' time."

Eleanor patted her arm. "I understand. I won't go either if you prefer. We can do another girl's night. What do you think, Jem?"

It took Jemma a moment to respond. "We should go and dance our hearts out. If people expect you to cry in the corner, do the opposite."

She sat forward in her chair excitedly. "How about we get people to sign up for a concert in aid of all those who have lost someone?"

Eleanor and Mel exchanged glances now. "Why is my stomach telling me it's a bad idea?" Mel asked, arms folded and brow wrinkled.

"Because you lost your sense of adventure when you lost your ability to ask out boys you like!" Jemma retorted and stuck out her tongue.

Mel sat back in her seat and waved her hand for Jemma to continue.

"Well, you had fun singing and dancing. It helped you to come out of yourself. It may work for others. We should at least sound out the idea with others and see what response we get." Jemma looked at them both expectantly.

The noise and bustle of the cafeteria kept going around them, and none of them spoke. Jemma bristled in annoyance. If they didn't like the idea, they could just tell her.

A group of older students sat down at the table next to them, jostling the girls out of their reveries.

"We could do it," Mel admitted grudgingly. "But where? And who would you invite to watch the performance?"

Jemma had already thought about this. "We could ask for permission to use Mark Billingsly Memorial Park. That way we can make it available to the families of our classmates."

"Hey," wailed Eleanor, "I thought this was supposed to be an addition to the school dance?"

"What if the school dance became the after-party? Or how about the day after? It's the last day of the school year." Jemma's mind raced to try to keep up with all the ideas flooding into her brain.

"So, you want us to ask for permission to use the park for a concert? For a few hundred people? To come watch a group of kids sing and dance?" Mel's tone remained unconvinced.

"Why don't we ask a member of staff if it's possible?" Eleanor countered.

"If we don't have a firm plan," Jemma asserted, "they won't take us seriously."

Mel looked at Jemma. "Jem, I'm not entirely sure I take us seriously."

Jemma's face fell. She'd really hoped the other two

would be up for this project. Her friends, seeing her distress, rallied.

"Since we need permission, if we head to the park after school and create a plan, we'll have something we can show the staff member," Eleanor offered.

"Sounds good." Mel nodded her agreement.

"Sure," Jemma replied despondently, staring down at her tray of food.

They finished their lunch in an awkward silence.

QBBS *Meredith Reynolds*, Mark Billingsly Memorial Park

The girls made their way to the park after school. It took them a few minutes to find a quiet space to sit and make their plans.

"I love it here." Mel sighed, looking around. "It's always so peaceful."

"Yes, and I love seeing the dogs when they are here." Eleanor looked around for Ashur or Bellatrix or the puppies. They weren't in the park today, and she looked disappointed.

"Okay, we need to get serious about this," Jemma started, bringing their attention back to their plans. She took her tablet from her bag. "Before we begin, where will the stage be?"

Mel pointed to a flat and slightly elevated location a few hundred yards away. "Over there would be a good place. We'd be higher than the crowd so they can see us more clearly. Plus, it means there are plenty of places for people to sit. If we are inviting families, they can bring picnics."

Eleanor asked, "Are we inviting just our year, or are we opening it up to the whole school?"

Jemma considered for a moment. "I think the whole school. I mean, even with their families, there's more than enough space."

"I've been thinking." Eleanor fidgeted with her sweater. "Why don't we make it a talent contest, combined with a charity concert?"

"I like it." Mel smiled. "People can show their support for families who have lost loved ones. Let's include *all* who have lost their lives, not just the military. For example, this park's namesake."

Jemma's fingers moved across the tablet as she logged their ideas. "Okay, so we need to ask permission to use the park. We also need someone to help us with staging the concert. We could ask Miss Harrison. I know she has done the sound and lighting for school plays before."

"Not to mention she likes us," added Mel, and they all nodded.

Jemma looked hard at Mel. "What changed your mind?"

"As you said, people need hope. To know it's okay to smile again." She took a deep breath and looked into the distance. Jemma could see tears forming in her eyes. "I keep seeing my dad's face when he saw us singing and dancing. Did you know it was the first time he's laughed since before…"

Jemma thought she understood but decided it would be better if she let Mel finish baring her soul first. It sounded like she needed to talk.

Mel looked at her friends and continued, "He needed to have a reason to keep on living. He has me, but some people are alone. Who will bring a light to banish *their* dark demons?"

A look of surprise and worry flashed across Eleanor's face, and Jemma imagined the same expressions on her own. Mel had always been the slightly ditsy and easy-going member of the group, but now Mel appeared to be introspective. They sat in silence for a while, letting the melancholy overwhelm them.

"Then let's *give* them hope," whispered Jemma.

Her determination washed away their sadness. "What will our performance be?" Eleanor asked, no longer fidgeting with her sweater. Her eyes sparkled as she asked the question.

"Well, we all know the words and dance moves to one song really well. I think there are a few others that we could learn over the next week," Mel mused. "So, I guess we need to practice for the performance."

"Yeah, let's choose three songs so that each of us has one song where we are the main singer," Eleanor suggested.

Jemma updated her notes. "Okay, and what shall we call ourselves?"

"How about we be a tribute band for the Empress, Gabrielle, and Tabitha?" Mel began. "We can dress up like them, with wigs and contact lenses."

"That doesn't answer what we should call ourselves," Jemma pointed out.

Eleanor giggled, and Jemma and Mel both snapped their heads around to look at her with a question in their eyes.

"Sorry, I just thought how they are all women, and that

they have very…noticeable features." She mimed a well-endowed figure. "I'm thinking, The Mamas and the Ta-Tas? I'm sure we can find enough tissues to complete the look."

Mel and Jemma were at a loss for words, then they broke into the biggest grins. "Excellent," and "Perfect," they exclaimed simultaneously

"I think we need to have the different acts audition so that the concert doesn't run too long," Jemma suggested.

"Good idea. How about we make posters to advertise the auditions for the concert? Then have one mega poster with tear-off tabs with audition times. It'll indicate whether people are interested," Mel said.

"I can make those," Eleanor volunteered. "What should we call the concert?"

Mel brightened. "How about 'A Concert to Remember?'"

"Ooh, that's clever," Jemma chimed.

"What is?" Eleanor looked confused.

"Well, we want people to remember to come to the concert." Mel raised a finger. "We want them to remember the concert after it's over." She raised a second finger. "Finally, we want people to come to the concert to remember those who have fallen." Mel waved three fingers.

"It's perfect," Jemma and Eleanor agreed in unison.

After a few minutes of making notes about their plans, Jemma looked up at her friends. A wave of nervousness made her doubt their plans for a moment.

"What if nobody comes?" worried Jemma.

"Then the concert isn't for them." Mel squeezed

Jemma's arm and flashed a warm smile. "We're doing this for those who need it."

"Then let's make the posters to show Miss Harrison tomorrow." Jemma smiled at her friends, and they returned to her apartment to complete their plans.

QBBS *Meredith Reynolds*, High School, Tuesday

When they got to school the next day, they went to see Miss Harrison immediately. They explained what they wanted to do, and showed her what they had put together so far.

"I'm impressed." Miss Harrison scanned their plans. "You've given yourselves two weeks to pull this together, but are you sure that's enough time?"

"Yes, Miss Harrison, if we get others involved, we should be able to prepare in time. Will we be able to use the park?" Jemma hoped the answer would be yes.

"I will make a request on your behalf. Since it's a charity event, I imagine you'll receive permission." She finally looked up at them and smiled. "I look forward to seeing the acts. As for backstage operations, I can organize a team to help you."

The girls left her office with excitement. They put up the posters before their first class, pinning their audition poster to the main bulletin board near the principal's office.

Impatiently they went to their first class, hoping it would pass quickly.

When the lunch bell rang, they ran to the main poster to see how many people would be auditioning at the end of the week. They skidded to a stop beside the bulletin board.

What they saw shocked them. Not one of the slips remained.

"I can't believe it!" Jemma checked around to make sure the slips hadn't been ripped off and thrown on the floor.

"Do you think somebody's messing with us?" Mel wondered.

Jemma felt sick but tried to sound confident. "I'm sure this is legit. I guess we'll find out in three days, since the auditions are on Friday."

QBBS *Meredith Reynolds*, High School, Friday

Audition day dawned, and the girls got to school early. They went straight to the audition room to get it ready for after school. Miss Harrison had sent them a message saying it would be available all day for them to set up.

They marked an area to indicate the stage space available on the night of the concert. They had registration forms so people could fill in the details of their acts, and the girls could record how long they took.

A growing buzz of anticipation followed them around the school all day, their classmates eager to learn about the auditions.

Jemma barely listened to her lessons, but none of the teachers reprimanded her. *How kind*, she thought. A few of the teachers stopped her during the day to wish her, Mel, and Eleanor luck with choosing acts. Some of them asked if they could help them prepare for the concert. The offers touched Jemma.

When they arrived at the door to the audition room, the corridors were silent. Students and staff were eager to start their weekends. Jemma recalled that only a week ago, she and Eleanor had rushed to Mel's quarters to give her support after the memorial. *What a difference a week makes*, she mused.

Looking nervously at each other, they reached for the door, pushing it open. The room bustled noisily.

Inside were almost forty students, half of them preparing for their auditions—tuning their instruments, getting into costume, or warming up their voices. The other half were there to cheer on their friends, and they chatted in anticipation.

Jemma felt tears prickling her eyes and swallowed the lump in her throat.

"Hey, guys, shut up! They're here," Owen shouted from the middle of the room. Everyone faced them and fell silent. Jemma broke out in a cold sweat, her insides squirming.

Holding their heads high, they walked to the stage to start the proceedings.

"Hi, all," Jemma started nervously. "Thanks for coming."

The crowd erupted into cheers and wolf whistles, and she blushed.

"Yes, well," she stammered. "You've seen the posters; the concert is in a week. The aim of today is for you guys to introduce your acts and give us a rough idea how long you'll need to set up and perform."

Mel continued, "We have three hours allocated for the entire performance, so we all need to be efficient when setting up. In fact, if any of you are willing to help others set up, please let us know."

Eleanor held up a form. "At the front are a stack of forms. Please fill out one per act. We need your names, what you want to call your act, and what you plan on performing. Leave the timing boxes empty; we will fill those in as you audition. Bring the form to the stage when you start your audition."

Excitement and anticipation filled the room. Jemma waved her hand at the stage as she gazed at the audience. "Who's first?"

The auditions filled her with the joy and hope she had wanted. *Oh my god, this is going to be awesome.* Judging by their grins and laughter, her friends' thoughts matched hers.

The first act was a group of five students performing circus acts, tumbling, juggling, and twirling flaming-batons. The last caused Jemma some concern, but it proved unfounded. The performance went exceptionally well.

Next came two jocks singing Rossini's cat duet, *Duetto buffo di due gatti.* Apparently, they were already working on their cat costumes. As the battle of the duet rose in crescendo, laughter, whistles, and applause filled the auditorium. The boys, Joey and Greg, bowed deeply to the room and sauntered off the stage.

As they reached another group of performers, one asked Joey, "Hey, aren't you afraid of being laughed out of school? Why are you doing it?"

Joey looked at him in confusion. "It's for a worthy cause."

Leaving the other boy in silence, Joey followed Greg to a seat to watch the next act.

The boy who took center stage looked small and timid. He stood fidgeting with his fingers, and Jemma gave him a smile of encouragement. He took a deep breath and began, in a voice far deeper and more sonorous than she expected, "It little profits that an idle king…"

The room listened, captivated. Jemma was sure she could have heard a pin drop in the silence. Everyone hung on his every word, and at the end stood to applaud his narration. The boy bowed awkwardly, his cheeks pink, and scurried from the stage.

Next came a couple of students who treated the room to a demonstration of their sleight-of-hand tricks, swiftly followed by a group of dancers who performed a variety of choreographed numbers to classical music.

A group of six took the stage, laughing and joking as they got into position. Their faces became somber, and they began a recitation of a work by William Shakespeare. They broke it up into pairs of lines and came together for the last couplet. "Once more unto the breach, dear friends, once more…"

Their words echoed around the silent room. The group finished in raised voices, bowed with flourishes, and bounced from the stage.

Finally, Owen and his three friends took the stage. They had set their instruments up already. Owen had a cheeky grin on his face and stood at the front.

"We," he indicated the band, "are The Bitches, and we are going to rock your minds."

The drummer and guitarist began to play, and Owen started singing a rock ballad made famous by Queen, promising that, "We will rock you." The room erupted into mayhem, and they all sang along. Owen strutted his stuff across the stage, winking at girls and encouraging everyone to join in. A brief break and they led straight into another Queen song, proclaiming to the room, "We are the champions." Once they finished, Owen said, "We want to include another song, but we can't decide what track to choose. Can we decide that night?"

An expectant silence gripped the room. Mel answered immediately, "Sure," and he gave her a dazzling smile.

"Well, thank you all for coming. You have been amazing," Jemma began. "From the conversations we've had during your auditions, I think we all agree there is enough time available for everyone on the night." Cheers met her words, and a lot of happy faces grinned at her.

Mel spoke up. "If we meet after school every day, we can plan scenery, lighting, sound, and anything else you might need. Enjoy your weekend, because next week is going to be brutal."

"But fun," came an anonymous shout from the crowd, followed by laughter.

The students left chatting happily and soon Jemma, Mel, and Eleanor were alone.

"Wow." Eleanor puffed out a breath.

"Yeah," marveled Mel.

Rushing in to hug them, Jemma exclaimed, "This just got real. If you guys come over tomorrow, we can finish the plans and practice our act."

"Sure," they agreed, and they all went home.

QBBS *Meredith Reynolds*

ADAM?

>>**How may I help you, Meredith?** <<

There's something you and Bethany Anne need to see.

Jemma, Mel, and Eleanor clattered noisily through the milling crowd of performers as the girls charged toward the stage curtain. Earlier in the day, Miss Harrison had sectioned off the area for the performers. It led directly to the stage and gave them a little privacy during the show.

They all wore dark trousers or shorts and tight dark tops. They had decided in the end to keep their figures natural since they would be running around a lot. As one of them had said, "A missing Ta-Ta would be hard to explain."

Mel wore a black wig and red contact lenses to look like Bethany Anne, and Jemma wore a chestnut-brown wig and brown contact lenses to look like Gabrielle. Eleanor wore a blond wig with black ends and a fake nose piercing, and they had drawn henna tattoos on her to make her look like Tabitha. They would be the first act and introduce the concert.

"Let's hope somebody turned up," Jemma said to the other two, who nodded their agreement. "Are we ready?"

"As ready as I'll ever be," admitted Mel.

"No, but let's do it anyway," squeaked Eleanor.

They pushed open the curtain and stopped in their tracks.

People filled the entire park. From where they stood, there wasn't a single space left. A group in the crowd spotted them and pointed them out to those around them. The news that the concert was starting passed like a ripple through the crowd, and the cheers and clapping rose in a deafening crescendo. The intensity of the noise made

Jemma's knees tremble, and for a moment she wanted to run.

Miss Harrison hurried over to them. "Oh girls, isn't this amazing?"

None of them spoke. Jemma wondered if they felt as overwhelmed as she did.

"Turns out," Miss Harrison continued, "your invitation of 'All Welcome' went viral." She gasped, "There are people in other areas of the base watching via video-link since there's nowhere to stand in the park."

Jemma finally found her voice. "How… I mean, why… I mean, who…"

Miss Harrison looked at her with pity. "Doesn't matter, dear. The hope you had planned to give will just affect a much larger group of people."

Jemma gulped and wished she could go back to her room and hide under the bedclothes.

"Come on, girls, you can do this. On the stage, you go." Miss Harrison chivvied them along.

The three looked out over the crowd once they got to the front of the stage. Then, positioning a microphone near her mouth, Jemma began, "We would like to thank you all for coming. In the next three hours, you will see a variety of performances. We have singers, dancers, acrobats, actors, and many more who will share their talents with you."

The crowd cheered her words.

Mel stepped forward and motioned to Jemma to let her speak to the audience. Jemma handed the mic to her with a smile.

Mel returned the smile and mouthed, "Get ready."

Eleanor and Jemma stood slightly behind her waiting to begin.

"My two friends and I are the Mamas and the Ta-Tas, and we will be starting the evening's festivities with a few songs. Some of you may know them, so please sing along if you do." She nodded to Miss Harrison, who started the music.

The girls struck a pose, hands clasped as if in prayer in front of them, as the first chords of the song pealed from the speakers. They held it until the first line of Madonna's *Like a Prayer* rang out in Mel's clear voice, then fell to their knees to match the lyrics.

It had been difficult to choose their second song. In the end, they had decided on Cindy Lauper's *Girls Just Wanna Have Fun* and now acted out the lyrics as best they could. The third song had just felt right. It had been Mel's mum's favorite, and the girls knew it well. They launched into Beyoncé's *Single Ladies*, pointing to their ring fingers and following the choreography from the original music video.

By the time the music ended on the third song, they were smiling, breathing heavily, and tired. They bowed to the audience, and Jemma stepped forward to introduce the next act.

"Ladies and gentlemen, I am pleased to announce our very own Cirque de Meredith."

Onto the stage acrobats tumbled, weaving and dodging and never touching each other. The crowd cried out with oohs and ah's in appreciation of their skill as they juggled and twirled the flaming batons. The performance came to a graceful end.

Eleanor came back onto the stage once the acrobats had

removed themselves and their props. "It gives me immense pleasure to introduce to you our favorite defensive tackle and quarterback, who have prepared for you a special rendition of Rossini's *Cat Duet*."

Onto the stage came Greg and Joey, dressed in cat costumes complete with ears and tails. In the highest voices they could reach, they sang the duet. The crowd laughed, cheered, whistled, and clapped. The boys threw themselves into the performance, drawing energy from the crowd and playing up the song.

It ended to thunderous applause, and the boys grinned at each other. Turning to the audience, they bowed theatrically before leaving the stage.

Jordan took center stage looking just as small and timid as he had last week. Again, Jemma gave him a smile of encouragement as she came on stage to introduce him.

"Without further ado, please welcome Jordan as he reads for us *Ulysses* by Alfred, Lord Tennyson."

The crowd became silent for the first time to hear the young boy. Jordan took a deep breath and began, his voice steady and his confidence growing with every sentence of his recitation. Until he reached the culmination,

"Tho' much is taken, much abides; and tho'

We are not now that strength which in old days…"

When he finished, the crowd, which had been silent, burst into tumultuous applause. The boy bowed, and as he left the stage, the girls saw that he had tears streaming down his face. Joey grabbed him in a bear hug and said, "You did good, Buddy. You did good."

Wiping her own eyes, Mel took to the stage once more, introducing the Magicians. There followed a colorful display of disappearing items, card tricks, and illusions. The crowd laughed and applauded its approval.

Miss Harrison came to the stage. "Ladies and gentlemen, we will now have a brief interlude. We will begin again in twenty minutes."

The crowd began to talk amongst themselves and avail themselves of the refreshments stands.

"What the..." The girls hadn't organized any refreshments. Jemma inquired, "Miss Harrison, where did these stands come from? We didn't plan for them."

"Funny thing. When I arrived earlier, the stall-keepers were setting up. Said they had heard about the show and wanted to show their support by offering refreshments. There are food and drink vendors. All Guns Blazing has a stall, and they are offering official merchandise." She indicated the stall to Jemma, Mel, and Eleanor, who gazed around in fascination.

"This is insane," muttered Mel.

"Way more than I'd ever imagined," replied Jemma.

Eleanor stayed silent.

After twenty minutes, they were all refreshed and ready to continue with the concert. The crowd settled as Jemma introduced the next act.

"Welcome back. Next, we have a display of modern dance. Please give a round of applause for Spatial Awareness." The crowd tittered.

The lithe dancers carried out the superb choreography. They wove a tale with their moves, which brought the music to life. From Pachelbel to Tchaikovsky, they stole the heart of the crowd. They bowed and curtsied to the cheering audience as they left the stage.

Eleanor bounced onto the stage. "Our penultimate act is none other than six members of Miss Harrison's English Lit class. Tonight, they will perform for you a scene from *Henry V*."

The six took to the stage more serenely than the previous week and stood apart as the rear of the stage took on an orange glow. In the background was heard the boom of cannons and the distant cries of men at war. They were lit by individual spotlights as they read their couplets, delivering a rousing speech and a call to war. The crowd, silent, hung on their every word. When at last they reached that final couplet, they announced together,

"Follow your spirit, and upon this charge

Cry 'God for Harry, England, and Saint George!'"

The sounds died away and the glow was extinguished, leaving the stage in darkness. The crowd roared its approval and the lights came up to reveal the students, who bowed, first to the audience and then to their comrades in the wings.

The audience cheered and called for more. The girls let the moment linger before stepping out together. It gave the final band a chance to get themselves ready.

"We would like to thank you all for your support this evening. You have been *amazing*," Jemma began.

"We hope you have enjoyed yourselves as much as we have," Eleanor continued. The crowd shouted its agreement.

"Please welcome our last act of the evening," Mel finished. "I will allow *them* to continue their introduction."

As the crowd settled, the band started to play simple chords and beats, and Owen stepped forward, looking like

John Grimes. Mel sighed in appreciation. The girls eagerly watched from the edge of the stage, wondering which songs they had decided to perform.

"Good evening, everyone. Have you had fun tonight?" he shouted into his mic. The crowd roared in response.

"Well, we are The Bitches, and we're here to rock your minds." He beckoned to the band, and they began to play. Power cords worthy of Queen rang out, and Owen led them through *We Will Rock You* and *We Are the Champions*.

They gave the crowd a moment to settle, and then once again Owen stepped forward with a glint in his eye and a grin on his face.

The drums were struck, the guitar thrummed, and Owen began to sing AC/DC's *Big Balls* in an affected British accent. The crowd went wild.

They jumped, they screamed, and they chanted along with him, getting louder at the chorus.

"Oh, my God!" Eleanor squealed, "Look who's in the front row."

They all looked. There were the Queen's Bitches, singing along with the rest of the crowd.

"Hell, yeah," shouted Jemma. "This just got epic."

Mel looked at her with big eyes. "It wasn't epic before?"

Jemma pointed at the men whose job it was to guard the most powerful woman in the Empire. "It doesn't get more epic than them. Except, of course, if the Empress herself had come. Which would never happen. So, *epic!*"

The girls laughed and joined in with the crowd.

After The Bitches finished their last song, the girls came onto the stage to thank them for their performance.

"We'd like to once again thank all our performers. I

think you'll agree with us that they've been awesome," Jemma yelled to the crowd. The roar of approval deafened those on the stage.

Mel waved them to silence. "As you know, we organized this concert to remember the fallen—any member of the Empire who lost their life in service to the Empress. We also wanted to remember their families and let them know they are not alone. So, will you all please join us in a minute's silence?" The instant she finished speaking, the park fell silent. *This is eerie,* Jemma thought, *but we did it. Kelly, if you are watching, Mel did it.*

As soon as the minute ended, the four men who had stood at the front of the crowd climbed onto the stage. Three of them held small boxes. John, Eric, and Scott came to stand in front of the girls and presented each of them with a box.

"The Empress would like to offer you these gifts as a reward for your hard work and generosity," the real John Grimes announced loudly as he handed his box to Jemma. She looked down to see the most exquisite pair of shoes in a Perspex box. On the front, a plaque read, Those who act out of kindness shall receive kindness in return. Bethany Anne, Empress of the Etheric Empire.

She looked up at the giant man, tears streaming down her face. She was speechless. After a moment, she turned to look at her friends, whose expressions mirrored her own.

The fourth man walked to where Owen stood. Darryl leaned over and whispered in the boy's ear. The boy's face went pale, and then he broke into a grin. Darryl gently pushed him toward the girls and Owen walked over to them. When he reached Mel, without a word, he put his arms around her and kissed her gently on the lips. Mel froze for an instant in surprise, then melted into the kiss. The crowd once again roared its approval.

Jemma and Eleanor hugged each other happily, setting their boxes down at the side of the stage. They retrieved Mel's, allowing their friend to get more comfortable with Owen. The kiss ended, and they both turned red-faced to the audience.

John whispered in Jemma's ear, "You may want to stand back."

Confused, Jemma took a step back and motioned for her friends to follow suit.

She blinked, and suddenly in front of her stood Empress Bethany Anne, Gabrielle, and Tabitha. The three women smiled at the girls, who were still made up as them. Gently, John, Scott, and Eric led Owen to the rear of the stage, leaving the women alone.

Bethany Anne stepped forward. "What do you say, girls? How about we give them an encore?"

The music started, and the six smiled and faced the crowd. As the first line of *Single Ladies* rang out, they raised their arms and began to dance.

The End

So, you know those days when you wake up, and you have a wonderful idea? Well, the first thing you do is put it on Facebook, right? That's what happened with this story. So social media is good for us, yeah?

Seriously, though, thank you to everybody in Fans Write who read my post and encouraged me to turn it into so much more. This story is for you.

I hope you had as much fun getting to know these three girls and their classmates as I did.

If you enjoyed the story and want to read more of my work I have recently released *First Comes Chaos*, the first book in my *Rexan Discovery* series. Book two, *Then Comes Silence* will be out soon. The links below are for my website and author page on Facebook, where I post information on upcoming projects.

Samantha Harmer

samanthaharmer.co.uk
https://www.facebook.com/SamanthaHarmerAuth
or/

HAIKU FROM THE KURTHERIAN UNIVERSE

Ashur and puppies.
Typical bewildered male.
Sympathy? Hell, no.

———

Yollins and Jotuns,
Noel-nis, Shimmers, and Yaree.
Wondrous universe!

DEATH AND NEW BEGINNINGS

BY T.L. GRYFEN

After Beth's world ends, can the sudden appearance of a long-discarded dream give her the strength she needs to carry on?

Beth Williams finds herself alone and heart-broken on the *Meredith Reynolds.* Unlike the majority of the residents, she feels she has nothing concrete to offer to the cause after they leave Earth. After a forgotten dream reappears during a medical treatment, she has to find the strength to accept her new reality and keep going.

Will she be able to bring herself to accept this new challenge and fight to keep it?

Dedicated to my mom and dad, Gail and David Notestine.

Without you both, I would never have had the courage to chase this dream. We miss you dad!

— Tracie

DEATH AND NEW BEGINNINGS

She stands intensely gazing through the window into the depths of space, strong, silent, and straight. The remains of ravaged beauty are visible on her face and in her once-well-groomed clothing and hair. As people push past on their way elsewhere, living their lives, she is alone. There is a large space around her, an intangible field that nobody dares cross. Her hands clench, small rivulets of blood just starting to slowly trickle past her tense white fingers. She speaks quietly to an image only she can see, somewhere in the dark void that stares back at her.

"Damn it, Steve, how could you do this to me? How could you bring me up here, to space for God's sake, and then leave me alone to cope with it? What am I supposed to do now? How could you be so stupid? You knew you had a malt allergy? Why did you have to ignore the warning signs? Did you think you were invincible? Just because the Queen and her Bitches are damn near immortal, didn't mean you were. I know you were so excited when Tom and Jeff asked you to work on their Artificial Intelligence program with them, you always loved technology, and this was something you had always dreamed of doing. You had gotten bored, semi-retired in a tiny Appalachian town, with nobody to relate to you, just me for company. I wasn't very good company, was I? Not recently at least, not while I was sick. But this, you just had to go back down to Earth without me. Why the hell were you in Ireland anyway? You had an allergic reaction and collapsed too far away from help to get you back up here to the *Meredith Reynolds*, too far away for a Pod-doc to save your life. How stupid, after everything we have done, to lose you to anaphylactic shock. You snuck away while I was getting my first gene therapy, and I lost you." She pauses, gathering herself, fighting to keep the sobs contained; praying that nobody passing will notice the tears.

"You said this was our next great adventure, that we had explored everything on Earth that we wanted to; hiked the pyramids, dove the seas of the Caribbean, explored the Southwest, traveled with gypsies, mined in Appalachia, and now it was time to explore off-world, to see what wonders we could find out there, together. We were supposed to do this together, and now you're gone, and I can't remember how to breathe!" another pause, another struggle for calm and equilibrium, another prayer for strength.

"The Queen offered to send me back home, said I didn't have to stay onboard or leave Earth with them, but how could I go back? Why do I care about going back to Earth? You aren't there, you aren't anywhere, so it's not home anymore. Lynne is here, and she is the only family I have left. I don't know how to keep living without you. I wake up in the middle of the night, reach for you, and you aren't there.

"You were my world, and now my world is gone. What am I supposed to do here on a spaceship? You and Lynne were the science fiction fanatics; I preferred a nice sitcom instead. You were the one who convinced me that this was a bold new step into the future. That we could do anything together, including starting a new life in a new galaxy. Once we leave the solar system, I don't have any useful skills to offer. I'm sure the Queen won't need a PR or marketing specialist in space. I can do my job promoting TBQ from Earth. The only reasons I was working from here were that this was where your job was, and for my treatments.

"This started out so well, you and Lynne were working together, and for once not trying to kill each other. I could see you finally trusting that she actually *did* love you. That she didn't resent you. That no matter whose blood she had, you were her father. You were finally accepting that us loving you wasn't a trap or some weird trick we were playing on you. But then you had to go and die. You had to leave me here with my heart ripped out of my chest and no breath in my lungs, just going through the motions."

Finally, she could hold the pain in no longer, and she collapsed against the window, tears pouring down her cheek and streaking the glass. Her strength lay in ruins around her.

From across the concourse, Lynne watched her mother quietly crumble. It had been three months since her stepdad passed away, and her mother was slowly falling apart. There was nothing she could say or do to change it. She was helpless in the face of such shattering pain. Lynne glanced down at the sleeping silver-furred bundle she clutched in both arms and whispered to the EI loaded into her tablet, "Are you sure about this, Zeus? She can barely take care of *herself* right now. She is never going to be able to take care of a puppy as well. I don't know what I was thinking, letting you convince me to do this."

"He is Steve's last gift to your mother. She deserves the chance to decide if she is going to accept him. Maybe it will help. You've had your work, immersing yourself in finishing what Steve started. You finished creating me, even started new projects, so you have had distractions from your grief. Your mother is alone on the *Meredith Reynolds* except for you. Arranging for your mother to get that puppy on the date of her last appointment was the last thing your stepfather did before dying. You owe it to both of your parents to finish what he started. Maybe now she'll even understand why he was in Ireland."

Suppressing tears of her own, Lynne reluctantly agreed. "How did you get so smart? You're younger than this puppy. You weren't even "born" until the day Steve died."

"I was programmed that way. ADAM made sure I had all the information I needed, and then even downloaded all of Steve's archives into my memory. It would be an insult to every one of you if I weren't this smart. "

Laughing through her tears, Lynne started towards her mother. "You know, I think we programmed *too* much of

Steve into you. You're just as much of a smartass, except ADAM made you even smarter, damn it. At least I could hold my own with him now that I'm an adult. I just wish Mom would let me install a terminal for you in her quarters since you're so much like him. It might make her feel better."

"Not yet, it wouldn't. She doesn't want reminders, she wants *him*, and no matter how much of him is programmed into me, I would only be a hurtful reminder."

"See, I told you that you were smarter than him. I loved him, but he wouldn't have thought of that." She snorted. "Actually, he would probably have said that you weren't *enough* like him. Not his voice, not his image. We did name you Zeus after the king of the gods, though. He would have gotten a kick out of that. That was the first computer program we ever worked on together." Lynne glanced towards the window, only to notice her mother walking away. "Shit! Where is she going?"

"She is meeting with Dr. Graeme for her last treatment. You might want to catch up with her. Oh, and don't let the puppy piddle on the decks. I am pretty sure that would not endear you to anyone, and you would have to clean it up."

"He's not gonna pee on the deck. He's housebroken. Come on, puppy." Lynne shifted him, draping his front paws over her shoulder and just supporting his hindquarters in her arms. "Let's try to catch your new momma before my arms fall off. Thank God you were the runt of your litter! I don't think I could carry you if you weighed as much as the rest of your littermates." Lynne hurried towards medical, complaining to her EI and the puppy the entire way.

Beth entered the medical office on automatic, answering the nurse's questions about her health and going through all the necessary motions of her final appointment. As she entered the inner office which contained the Pod-doc, she was still lost in her thoughts. The gene therapy she was undergoing was a miracle, possible only because of the alien technology that was the Pod-doc, but she honestly didn't care anymore. When she was first approved for the treatment, it had meant the opportunity to spend another lifetime with the love of her life. Now it just meant facing endless days without him. She had only completed the treatment at Lynne's insistence. Steve's death on Earth during the very hours she was receiving her first treatment had destroyed the miracle for her. The irony of losing her reason for living just as she regained the ability to live had come close to killing her.

"Beth? Beth, are you listening to me?"

" Hmmm? Oh, I apologize, Dr. Graeme. I was a million miles away. Could you repeat your question, please? "

"I asked how you were feeling? Have you had any issues since your last session five weeks ago? Any reduction in your energy levels or ability to sleep?"

" I've been having problems sleeping. I fall asleep just fine, I just can't *stay* asleep. I have nightmares every night. I wake up with panic attacks. But, that has nothing to do with the treatments or even any side effects, it's simply my life right now. So, should I start getting ready? "

"Yes, please. As you know, Beth, this is the last time you will need to come in. This last treatment is to finish cleaning out the junk code, as it were, from your DNA. It will also give you a quick rejuvenation, and install the implants you need to directly communicate with the *Meredith Reynolds* and the EIs in the different departments. Have you given any thought to what you want to do next?"

"I'm not thinking any farther ahead than the next hour. I am literally taking everything one step at a time."

"I understand. I'll leave you to get ready. Just put your clothes on the chair, and get into the Pod. I'll be back in a moment."

As Beth started to undress, she heard the door click behind her. Assuming it was Dr. Graeme leaving to give her privacy she ignored it, lost in her thoughts.

———

Lynne shoved the door of the doctor's office aside with her shoulder, saw the empty room, and sighed. "Am I too late, Dr. Graeme? I would have been here sooner, except we had to stop and sniff every new thing on the way." She gave the puppy an exasperated look as he licked her nose. " Can I put him down somewhere? He is really heavy. "

"Of course. The floor is tile, so he can't hurt it. Do you mind if I ask exactly why you are carrying around a puppy?"

Lynne bent down to put the puppy on the office floor and then addressed the doctor. "Steve bought him for Mom. He picked him out the day he went to the surface; that's why he went down there in the first place. The breeder called today. Meredith patched the call to me, and I went and got him. He was supposed to be a congratulations gift for finishing the treatments. That and an emotional support animal. I personally don't think she's ready, but Zeus is being a butthead and insisting I let Mom decide."

Dr. Graeme smirked. "I know you don't want to hear this, Lynne, but I actually agree. Your mom is lonely. I'm not a therapist, but I think that maybe having the puppy would help her. Give her someone and something to care for and talk to."

"That's what *I* said! "

Lynne gave her tablet a dirty look. "Nobody asked for comments from the peanut gallery, Zeus. Just hush." She chuckled. "I should never have programmed him with Steve's quirks. It seemed like a good idea when Dad was the one who would be dealing with him, but now that it's me, he loves pushing my buttons."

"Well, he *is* male, and you did have an interesting relationship with your dad. It makes sense that you would have an interesting relationship with his brainchild. Anyway, your mom was getting ready to go into the Pod-doc, so let me go get her settled. This last treatment should only take a few hours if you want to wait for her."

Dr. Graeme pushed open the door to the inner office. "Beth, are you ready? "

"I am. Let's get this over with. You keep your office freezing!"

"Go ahead and settle in. You know the drill. I will program your final treatment, and when you wake up, the last of your health issues will be cured."

Beth stepped into the Pod-doc and settled herself. This was the third time she had done this, so she did know how it worked. Soon, she would drift off to sleep, and then the changes to her DNA would be made. As she settled back and started drifting, she felt something warm and wet wrap around her ankle.

She just had time to think, "What the..." before everything faded to black.

The doctor watched the Pod-doc seal closed and turned to the control panel to finalize the program. As she was entering the treatment parameters, she could hear the sounds of furniture shifting around in the reception room, and Lynne's voice calling in a sing-song tone.

"Puppy? Where are you, you little monster? I know you're in here somewhere Liam. Dr. Graeme, have you seen the puppy?"

"No, I haven't. Let me look around in here." Dr. Graeme scanned the inner office, glancing at the Pod as she passed. "Uhm, Lynne? Could you come in here a minute? I found the puppy, but we have a slight...issue."

Lynne rushed in. "What is it? Is my mom ok?"

"Oh, she's fine, but I think that her accepting Liam is now a moot point. Look inside."

Lynne saw her mom reclining, the puppy curled around her legs with his head on her feet.

"Well, crap. Can we get him out of there?"

"No. We can't interrupt this final phase of the treatment. The puppy isn't going to interfere, but he *is* going to be enhanced and linked to your mom. I just need to make some tweaks to make sure he isn't hurt by the treatment. His genes don't need the same rewriting your mom's do."

"Wait a minute, *enhanced*? You mean like Ashur? Bigger, smarter, stronger, et cetera?"

"Yes."

"Oh, shit! We are all so screwed. Do you have any idea what kind of puppy that is? An Irish Wolfhound. Unenhanced, a full-grown male is over three feet tall at the shoulder. If that puppy is enhanced anywhere near the extent Ashur was, he is going to be a small horse. Think a Shetland pony with teeth and claws and puppyish enthusiasm." She collapsed on a nearby stool and put her head in her hands. "This should be interesting, to say the least. So, when are they going to be done? I don't guess that it's still only going to be a few hours?"

"No, they'll be out in two days. The treatment is going to be slowed down considerably since the Pod-doc will be almost rebuilding them both while keeping them separate. I strongly suggest that you come back then. I am not going to be the one who explains this to your mom. "

"No, I wouldn't expect you to be. I'll be back in two days. Don't let them out until I get here."

Lynne wandered out of the office, muttering to herself and her EI about monster-proofing her mom's quarters.

Two days later when Lynne arrived at the doctor's office, she was surprised to see a large crowd gathered, including a tall man in a Guardian's uniform.

"Uhm, is there something going on? What is everyone doing here?"

Dr. Graeme hustled over to her. "Lynne, don't worry. Most of these people are here because they are nosy. They want to see how big the puppy gets. Jay, the Guardian, is here to assist if things get out of control."

"I'm glad he is here, but honestly I'm actually concerned about my mom's reaction. She had the option of accepting my dad's gift before this happened, but now she is tied to that puppy. If what I have heard about the bond between the Queen and Ashur is accurate, my mom has no choice in the matter."

"She still has options, Lynne. The bond isn't life or death. Neither of them will die if they don't stay together."

"No, I know it isn't life or death, but they'll be able to feel each other's emotions right?"

" Well, yes, but... "

"No buts. You'll see what I mean. My mom is not going to handle this well. Now, can we get all of these people out of here except Jay? He can stay outside the door until I'm sure we don't need him. My mom may not be body-shy, but she isn't going to want all these people around when that Pod opens."

She stopped and looked around, then started trying to herd the crowd out of the room. Once it was clear, she turned back to the doctor. "I think we are ready. I really hope this goes better than I'm expecting it to."

"Ok, here we go. Fingers crossed." Dr. Graeme approached the Pod-doc and released the cover. She had no sooner stepped back when it surged open, and the puppy leaped out. Any doubt about the effect the enhancement would have on his size were put to rest, since his head now came up to the doctor's waist. The puppy propped his front paws on Beth's lap and started licking her face.

Beth surfaced slowly from her induced sleep. Something warm and wet was washing her face, and there was a substantial weight on her thighs.

Momma, Momma, come on! Wake up!

What?

Momma, you have to wake up and take me to sniff stuff. Sissy is here too, and she is waiting for you.

Beth sat straight up, shoving the weight off her lap. When she opened her eyes, she saw an oversized wolfhound puppy grinning at her feet, tongue flopped out and eyes smiling.

"*What the hell?*" She scrambled out of the Pod and away from the puppy, who tried to follow."No! You stay there! Somebody tell me what the hell is going on here. Where did that puppy come from, and why is he talking in my head?" Beth's voice increased in level with every word until she stood screaming in the corner farthest away from them all. The puppy jerked away from the noise in fear, knocking into Lynne and sending her to the floor. He wound up cowering in her lap, staring up at all of them. The door crashed open as Jay came rushing in. It closed behind him as he paused, seeing no danger.

Lynne murmured to the puppy for a minute, soothing him, before glancing up at her mother. "Mom, just calm down. I'll explain everything, but you need to get a grip. Why don't you get dressed? You'll feel better when you aren't naked." Lynne stayed on the floor, stroking the puppy overflowing her lap and waiting for her mother to finish dressing and sit down.

While her mom was dressing, Lynne started explaining. "Ok, so this beautiful boy is Liam. He is, well, *was*, a gift from Steve to celebrate the end of your therapy. He paid for him and picked him out the day he died. One of the breeders in Ireland had a litter that was about two weeks old, and they had more puppies than were spoken for. He explained to them that you were going through therapy and that we were all going to be leaving Earth with the Queen eventually. When he told them about all of your experience raising large dogs as well as rehabilitating rescue animals, they agreed to sell him the puppy." Lynne half-laughed, "I think they were kind of excited to possibly have one of their dogs be the first 'hound in space.'"

"No, Lynne, I can't. It's too much! Damn it! Just, *no*! How can I take care of a puppy? It's too much! I can't be responsible...You can't expect me to..."

Beth's voice got increasingly louder, the puppy cringing farther and farther down in Lynne's lap with every word until she finally interrupted, "Mom! Stop it! You are terrifying and hurting Liam!"

"What do you mean, I'm hurting him? I haven't gotten near him!"

"He's bonded to you, Mom! That means he can tell what you're feeling! He is thousands of miles away from his mother, his littermates, and the only home he has ever known, and you are rejecting him. He hears and understands you saying you don't want him. He loves you unconditionally, and you are telling him—showing him—that he isn't worth loving. If you would calm down for one fucking minute and pay attention to how you are really feeling and not just your knee-jerk reaction, you would feel how much he loves you."

Lynne paused to wipe tears from her eyes. "I get it, Mom.

You lost the love of your life, your reason for existing, just when you were starting to feel good again. You feel guilty that you were sick for so long, you are angry at him for dying, and you feel guilty about being angry. You feel alone, and you know I would take that away if I could. There isn't a day that passes that I don't wish it was me instead, because at least you would have him to help you through it, but that wasn't what happened." Lynne was on her knees now, facing her mother.

"I can't fix your loneliness, Mom, but Liam can. He loves you. You can actually *feel* how much he loves you, and he can talk to you. He is smart, and he is going to get even smarter as he grows up. You can talk to him. He will always be willing to cuddle, to play, to go on an adventure, or simply have a quiet time at home as long as he is with you. Most importantly, Mom, Liam was Steve's—was Dad's—last gift to you."

"Nobody expected things to work out the way they have, but this is what we have, and we have to deal with it! Just give Liam a chance. He is a sweetie, and we can all see that he already loves you so much!"

As Lynne was speaking, Beth had been sliding slowly down the wall. Now she was huddled in the corner, crying. Seeing her in tears, Liam left Lynne's side to tentatively approach Beth, and he carefully started licking away her tears.

Don't cry, Momma. I understand if you don't want me. I can stay with Sissy. She'll take care of me. Please don't cry. I love you, but you don't have to love me too.

With every word Liam projected Beth cried harder, and the puppy frantically licked away her tears, trying to stay ahead of the flow, pressing his body against her knees. Finally, Beth uncurled enough to put her arms around his neck, until she was half draped across him, crying into his fur.

Momma? You are getting my fur wet. Do you want me to go away with Sissy now? His ears and tail drooped as he started to pull away, looking dejected. Beth unconsciously tightened her grip on his fur, and he yelped. She let go with a start.

"Oh, Liam, I am so sorry, puppy. I didn't mean to hurt you. I didn't know..." she spluttered. Liam licked her face and wagged his tail slowly.

I'm okay, Momma. You didn't hurt me. Do you want me to stay?

"Yes, sweetie, I want you to stay. Maybe you can help me not be sad. I'm probably going to cry a lot, though. I lost somebody I loved, and I really miss him."

It's ok, Momma. I'll dry. Sissy told me you lost Daddy. I sort of remember him. I never saw him since my eyes were closed, but I remember he smelled really good, like fried chicken and sausages, and he had strong hands when he picked me up.

"Fried chicken and sausages, huh? He must have had lunch before he picked you out. But that's right, sweetie, I lost my husband, and I am sad. But you can help me, maybe. Now, I need you to go with Lynne—"

You said I could stay with you! Why do I have to go with her? I'll be good.

"You *are* good, baby, I just need her to take care of you while I buy what we need for you to stay with me."

Lynne interrupted her mother, "Actually, Mom, I

already bought everything you'll need. I've had a lot of time the last few days."

" How did you know I would keep him? "

"Are you kidding me? I know you! During my entire childhood, your pets ate better than we did. You love animals, and you have wanted a wolfhound for over a decade. One who could talk to you and understand English, who could actually tell you he loved you? I was pretty sure that if you could get past all of your made up reasons not to let him, he would be staying with you."

Lynne handed her mother a collar and leash. "I even bought him treats."

I like treats! Treats are yummy. Can I have treats?

"That's up to Mom, puppy. I'm sure if you are good she will give you treats. So, Mom, are you ready to take your puppy for a walk? He looks like he could use a tree, or at least a puppy pad."

Smart Sissy. Love Momma, but I really gotta go to the bathroom.

Liam stood fidgeting by the door, nearly shoving the forgotten Guardian out of the way in his eagerness.

Beth took the leash and collar from Lynne, leaning in to hug her daughter and kiss her cheek. "Thank you, pumpkin. I hope you know how much I love you and appreciate what you do for me. I miss Steve so much it physically hurts, but I would never trade you for him. I would be just as heartbroken."

"I know, Mom. I just feel so helpless sometimes. I can see you fading away in front of me, and I can't do a damn thing about it. Now, go walk your puppy before he pees on Jay."

Beth laughed, then after thanking everyone in the room for their help and apologizing for the upset, she left with Liam pulling on his lead in front of her.

Lynne watched with a smile as her mother was tugged from the room by the eager puppy, then turned to the other two people in the room.

"Thank you both so much. I apologize for the drama. Dr. Graeme, you have been fantastic. Everything you've done for my mom. I don't even know how to thank you. I truly appreciate you still making it work when Liam...injected himself into the Pod-doc. Not many people would have been able to take that in stride, complete my mom's treatment, and make sure it didn't damage the puppy."

She turned and addressed Jay, "I am truly grateful for you being here, and thank God you didn't have to be. I shudder to think what could have happened if Liam weren't such a sweet-natured puppy, or if my mom had continued to deny him. This place doesn't need an angry or depressed enhanced puppy the size of a pony running around."

Jay just smiled at her quietly. "It wasn't a problem. After dealing with the Marines and the Queen's Bitches, a puppy was child's play. I'm glad it worked out." He turned towards the door and then paused, turning back around halfway." I know you aren't thinking about it, but someone is going to need to brief the higher-ups about this. Liam could be dangerous at some point, even if he isn't now, and we all need to know what we're dealing with. "

"Wait a minute! Brief who, exactly, and why? He's a puppy, not a new weapon!"

"Yes, he's a puppy. An oversized puppy from a species

that was bred to take out packs of wolves, and that was at a normal size. That adorable puppy is already the size of a full-grown hound and has twenty-one months of growing left. I'm sorry, Lynne, but at a minimum, Peter and John are going to have to be briefed on him and his specific enhanced capabilities. "

Lynne collapsed back on to the floor. "I don't *know* his specific enhanced capabilities! *Mom* doesn't know his capabilities. Hell, *Dr. Graeme* probably doesn't even know his capabilities. Can't we just assume he has similar capabilities to Ashur and leave it at that?"

"The problem is, Ashur wasn't a puppy when BA put him in the Pod-doc. Nobody knows what will occur with an enhanced puppy. A lot of people are interested."

"Ok, Jay. I'll make sure my mom takes care of it." She turned to the doctor, "Dr. Graeme, Mom and I will be back tomorrow for you to do a follow-up with her and the puppy. Zeus, can you contact mom for me?"

"Of course, Lynne. What do you want me to say?"

"Just let her know that we need to be back here tomorrow."

Jay interrupted, "If you want, I'm sure you could bring him to the APA for us to run him through an obstacle course tomorrow. That way you get it all done at once."

"Thank you, Jay. We'll be there. Don't know what will happen afterward, but I guess we will see tomorrow."

The next day Lynne stepped hesitantly into the APA. She had picked up her mother and Liam bright and early and taken them both for medical testing. Now she had gone ahead to meet with the people who would be administering the puppy's physical testing. She had no idea what was going to happen, and it had her worried. Clearing the doorway, she looked around for someone she knew who she could speak to and spotted Jay talking to a large man in loose sweats. She headed toward him, shoving her way between them and speaking as she did.

"All right, Jay, Mom, and Liam are on their way. I still think this is stupid. What fool in their right mind would insist that my mom's puppy could possibly be a danger to anyone?"

"That would be me."

The deep voice came from above and behind her. She craned her head back to look at the speaker and gulped. "Fuck me, you're...you're John Grimes. *The* John Grimes, aren't you? Oh...my...God, the Queen isn't here, is she? I don't want to be here if this goes bad and my mom and the Queen both are here.

"I'm babbling. Oh Lord, I'm babbling at THE Queen's Bitch. someone shoot me now..." Lynne finally ran out of breath and paused for air, only then noticing that Jay and John were laughing at her. "I'm really not this much of a dork, I promise. I'm just worried. You guys aren't going to kill my mom's dog, are you? " John shook his head, eyes still laughing.

Jay answered her soberly. "No one is going to kill the dog, but...some sort of arrangements are going to have to be made."

"What kind of arrangements? Look, I know you guys don't get this, but the rest of us aren't as tough as you. She already lost my dad, and he was her life. If you take that puppy away from her, I think it might kill her." Lynne turned to greet her mom as she entered the room, leaving Jay and John to continue their conversation.

Beth entered the room with Liam bouncing beside her. There had been no real surprises in the doctor's office. She was fine, completely healthy, and with an extended lifespan due to the nanocytes used to fix her genes. Liam was healthy, currently thirty-eight inches tall at the shoulder, seven feet long from nose to tail-tip, with an expected final height of fifty inches and length of eight feet. His lifespan had also been extended as a result of the nanocytes, and she wouldn't have to worry about losing him for quite a few years. According to Dr. Graeme, he had the intelligence of an eight-year-old, which would mature to that of a young adult human. He had a sweet and even temperament and seemed eager to please. Now, they just had to get through this mysterious testing.

Momma, Momma, look! There's Sissy. Hi, Lynne!

He ran over to Lynne, chattering all the way. As he did, Beth looked around the room. There were strangers in military PT gear standing around the outskirts of the arena-sized space, as well a couple of well-dressed women in a viewer's area at the far end. On the floor itself, an obstacle course had been set up. It looked like a hybrid of a regular agility course and a Special Forces training course. As she glanced around, she noticed Dr. Graeme come in and start a conversation with one of the men in sweats.

Liam came running back. *Momma! Did you see? They have lots of stuff for me to play on, and I get to run and play tug-of-war with some of the soldiers. Some of them smell like doggies.*

Sissy says they are actually wolves. Do wolves walk on their back legs like humans do?

Beth laughed. "These do. Sometimes they are humans and sometimes they're wolves, though I've never seen it. So, any idea what else you're going to have to do?"

Lynne says she's gonna ask the really big guy. Then I get to play.

The puppy ran back towards Lynne, tripping over his paws and righting himself with a doggy grin. Beth laughed as she watched him run past her daughter to jump around Jay and the large man with him.

"Mom, do you have a minute? We need to talk. You are going to have to make some decisions soon."

"What do you mean? What kind of decisions?"

"This testing, once he completes it, is where they decide if he is a danger to society and the *Meredith Reynolds.* If they don't think you can control him until he learns better, they are going to take him away from you. That big man with Jay? That's John Grimes, and he's here to report back to the Queen. What he says goes, unless she contradicts him."

"So how do we stop it?"

"I don't know. I really don't, Mom. I don't know what the right answer is. I guess we just let Liam take the tests, which he seems to be excited about doing, and then worry about it. I might be worrying about nothing."

As Lynne and Beth watched, Jay crouched to talk to Liam, laughing as the puppy licked his face and chattered a mile a minute in his head. The two walked back to the women, with Jay resting his hand on the puppy's back.

"Ok, so here's how this is going to work. Beth, we want you to direct Liam through the agility course first. Don't worry about how he does or if he messes up. We just want to get a baseline on his natural speed and agility. This will also help us to judge how well you are communicating with each other, and how well he comprehends what you tell him. Then, he'll get to play tug of war with one of the Wechselbalg so we can test his strength, and with a machine so we can test his jaw power. Then, depending on the results of all of those tests, we'll have you send him through the obstacle course with me, and he will have certain tasks to do. Nothing will hurt him, and this should give us a good idea of how strong and smart he is. I know Dr. Graeme's testing indicated he is in perfect health, that his muscle and bone density increased to compensate for his added height and weight, and that he has the intelligence of an eight-year-old. We'll try and keep this fun for him, ok?"

"And then what, Jay? What happens when you have your results?"

"Then you decide what you are going to do. Whatever decisions are made, you will be a part of them."

Beth sighed. "Whatever, let's go, Sergeant. The sooner we get this over with, the better." She called Liam to her. "Come on, puppy, you get to go play now!"

Yay! This all looks like fun, Momma. Are you gonna play too?"

"Yes, sweetie, I am."

The two walked off to the start of the agility course.

ONE HOUR LATER...

Beth watched as Liam finished playing tug-of-war with a werewolf and shook her head. This was her life now.

Werewolves and vampires were real, she was on a spaceship designed using alien technology by people who worked for a vampire queen, and she was not only healed of a debilitating genetic disease but also enhanced with nanocytes to live into her hundreds.

She also had a gigantic wolfhound puppy who talked to her in her head. It sounded like the plot of a movie that Lynne or Steve would have watched. Her eyes teared up a bit as she thought of her husband. She couldn't believe he had gone and bought her a 'hound. She had wanted a wolfhound for more than a decade, but her health would never have allowed it. They had stopped discussing it years ago. It was so much like him to have bought her one, as a surprise once he knew she was going to be ok. Her thoughts were interrupted by Liam bouncing up to her.

Momma, did you see? I played tug of war with a wolf! I got to run around, and jump over stuff, and swim, and...

"I saw, sweetie. You did really good. Did you get any treats?"

Uh huh. Lynne gave me a hot dog and some cookies. I like treats. Can I have more? You helped me bunches. You told me where to go, and when to turn. Can we do it again?

"Maybe later, baby. Momma needs to talk to Jay right now. Come with me."

Ok, Momma. Then can we go outside? I miss the sky. I want to chase butterflies and roll around in the grass and lay in the sun..

Beth had already started heading toward John and Jay, but paused in thought for a minute at Liam's words. Walking up to the two men, Beth confronted John. "So, what's the verdict, Mr. Grimes? How'd he do? Are you going to try and take away my puppy?"

John opened his mouth to reply and was interrupted by Liam pushing between them.

You can't take me away from my momma! She needs me. I am hers, and she is mine. Daddy got me for her. You're a bad man! Liam started growling, raising his hackles at the startled man. Beth gripped him by the collar.

"Liam, stop. Nobody is taking you away from me, but you need to calm down now." Beth looked up at the men. "Go ahead."

Jay looked at John and answered, "There is some concern. He has the jaw strength of a great white, and that's now, as a puppy. He is just going to get stronger. When he gets older, he is going to be a match for a full-grown werewolf in Pricolici form. John thought...*we* thought...that it would be better if Liam stays here with the Guardians until we are sure he isn't going to hurt someone."

NO! I will not *leave Momma! Bad men! Bad men, to try to take me away. I will stay with her forever!* Liam lunged towards the men, barking and howling until Beth's hand on his collar brought him back.

"Liam, down. *Stay.* As for you two, you can see that isn't going to work. Liam is mine, and I am his, He will do much better being raised in a loving home by someone who has experience training large dogs than being raised by the military. If you want to make sure he isn't a danger to himself or others, then I need to make sure his sweet and loving nature is never ruined. You will take him away from me over my dead body." Beth stood between Liam and the two men, glaring up at John. "I don't care who you are, and I don't care what the Queen says. This puppy belongs with me!"

Jay started to respond and was interrupted yet again, this time by a slender brunette. "She's right, Sergeant. We're supposed to be the good guys. If at all possible, Liam needs to stay with his family. I think you can see by his reaction that he is already loyal to her."

Beth jumped. "Your Majesty! I didn't mean..."

BA laughed. "Can it, Beth. You meant every word. You would gladly spit in my face right now if you weren't afraid of what would happen."

"Only if I thought you were going to try to take Liam away from me. Otherwise, I would never disrespect you like that."

"And how are you going to take care of him? How are you going to make sure he doesn't accidentally hurt someone here on the ship? I have a lot of patience, Beth, but if that puppy hurts one of my people, you are *not* going to like my reaction." Bethany Anne's eyes glowed red for a second.

Beth began to respond angrily, but paused. When she started again, she was calmer. "Ok, those are good questions, although I'm not sure I deserved you vamping out on me. I actually do have an idea that might make all of us happy. The job I do for you is actually easier for me to do from Earth. The only reason I was on board was for my treatments, and for Steve's work. I have responsibilities on the ground that I have been ignoring, like handling the last of Steve's affairs. Liam misses the sky, and honestly, so do I. So, why don't I take him home? Back to North Carolina.

I can advertise and promote TQB from there, and train Liam. I have a lot of practice training large-breed dogs, and the theory is the same, no matter how much larger he is than normal. He still needs to be taught not to jump on people, and that biting is bad unless he is eating or protecting people.

"Actually, since he understands me, it will be easier. I can explain why certain behaviors are bad, instead of just teaching him that they are. I get that he is making you all nervous, even if I don't agree, so let me teach him on Earth in slightly less close quarters, where mistakes won't matter so much."

Beth paused and looked pleadingly at the Queen. "Let me do this, please?"

BA looked at her and then down at the puppy. "What do you think, Liam? Do you want to go back down to Earth?"

I get to stay with Momma?

"Yes. Nobody will separate you from your momma."

Yes! Let's go. I can show Momma my favorite trees, and the pond where I swim, and she can meet my brothers and sisters. Can we go now?

"I guess I have my answer. All right, Beth. Wrap up everything you have going on here, and then get with Cheryl Lynn to see what she is going to need from you while you are on the ground. This is not a permanent move. I will put a Pod at your disposal to get moved down. You will still be expected to come up periodically for meetings, and to show me how Liam is progressing. If this doesn't look like it's working, we'll figure it out then."

Beth smiled. "Yes, ma'am." She turned to Liam. "You ready to go get packed, baby? We are going to Earth."

Yes, Momma. I am ready. Let me just say thank you.

Liam ran around the room thanking everyone he had been "playing" with on the course with kisses and tail wags, finally stopping at BA. He gently placed his paw on her shoulder and licked her face. *Thank you for letting me stay with my momma. You are a nice lady. Okay, Momma, let's go.*

She stands intensely gazing through the Pod window into the depths of space, strong, silent, and straight. Her face is calm, the ravages of tears drying on her face. Beside her stands a large silver hound, her hand on his back. She speaks to an image only she can see, floating in the void outside the window.

"Well, Steve, I have my hound. I think we're closer than you could've ever imagined we would be. I miss you so much every day, but, it is getting better. Liam helps, and Lynne helps. I am going to be strong, and I will make it through this.

"Talking to Liam, spending my time with him and telling him about you, I remember the good times we had. I am going back to Earth to finish my job and take care of your estate. Lynne says she will come visit as often as she can, and I'll visit her when Liam and I come back for meetings and assessments. But Liam and I are going home. You would be proud of me. Of us."

Tears start trickling down her face. "I just wanted to say goodbye. I love you, Steve. I always will. Thank you so much for everything you gave me throughout our life together. I will always remember you, and our good times.

Lynne would make you proud. She finished your project, and she takes good care of me.

"I'm off on my next great adventure. You may not be by my side, but you are in my heart."

She turns away from the window, laughing as the dog jumps up to lick her face clean. "Thank you, Liam. I'm ready now. Sit down. It's time for us to go home."

The End

First, before anything, THANK YOU! Thank you for reading, and hopefully enjoying, my story. Thank you to the
Fans Write group members who read this story at the
beginning and encouraged me to continue. Thank you to
MA for letting us all play in his sandbox! A special thanks
to Erika and Sarah for helping me when the story had to
go in a slightly different direction.

 This story was written because I had to write it, plain
and simple. I started and never finished four other stories
for the Fans Write anthology before finally giving up and
writing this one. I lost my dad December 3rd of last year,
and no matter what story I tried to write, the grief and loss
made itself known so strongly that I had to get it out. So, I
shamelessly plagiarized my life. I took my grief, and my
mom's grief, and shoved us all onto the *Meredith Reynolds*.
Oh, and I added a dog—a silly oversized puppy to make us
all smile.

 This is not the first story I have written. It's not even

the first thing I have ever had published. It is, however, the first time I have written something so intensely personal to me and then shared it with the world. Something that would not allow me to leave the pages blank.

This is my dream. It *has* always been my dream! I have so many stories, whole universes even, inside my head waiting to get out. This is my first attempt at sharing those stories, those voices inside my head, with anyone but my closest friends and family, so thank you for being my guinea pigs!

I have heard it said that writers write because they have no choice. There is something inside us that will not be silenced, no matter how hard we try. I think this is true, and when we are very lucky; that something—that voice, if you will—lives on long after we die. Thank you for listening to my voice.

This has been scary, fun, and thrilling, kind of like a roller coaster ride. I hope it continues.

Ad Aeternitatem!

Trae

HAIKU FROM THE KURTHERIAN UNIVERSE

Wrinkle-assed ball-sack,
Llama-sniffing fudge packer.
Who thought of those, Mike?

———

John, Eric, Scott, Darryl,
BA has a badass team.
The Queen's Bitches rule!

———

ADAM and TOM try
to impart sense to BA
Thankless job, ain't it?

THE VALLEY

BY KAT N. SNOW

In a world turned upside down, some people just kept on living a normal life, without a clue what was going on outside what they knew. Most of them never realizing that there was something different about a neighbor, or an acquaintance. Asa could be your best friend if you needed one, but don't get on her bad side, you won't like what can happen because she is different. What do you know about the people that live near you?

CHAPTER ONE

The drone of many people talking was getting louder, and Asa was getting a headache. She stood with her elbows on the bar and her chin in her hands, looking bored and half-asleep. It seemed as though she were paying no attention, but she was really watching several of the people closely between pouring drinks. Lexi had just grabbed a tray full of cider and was turning away as one guy shoved another, knocking him into her. Asa took the tray with one hand, pulling Lexi to the side with the other. It happened so fast that Lexi barely realized what had happened. She turned to yell at the guys, but they were just standing there looking at each other like they had never intended to fight. Asa handed Lexi back her tray, smiled, and didn't say a word. It was easier that way.

Normally there weren't this many people. They had been streaming in since the rains and snowmelt from the mountains had started flooding the lower lands. While that made for very fertile land, most years it brought lower levels of water. This year was particularly heavy. Asa's place was on a hill, so it didn't have the problem some of the rest of the valley did. Many people built their homes on stilts because they'd lost one to the water once. Others like Asa got lucky and were rarely affected by the floods.

The inn was fairly large. The kitchen was in the back, and there were smaller rooms upstairs and two more rooms downstairs. The main room was public and furnished with a dozen tables and benches. It was near many farms and homes, and people often came in to ask for a room or camping space while they did their business.

Asa didn't charge them. She really couldn't. Most people paid with goods because they hadn't had or used money in a very long time. Rarely they paid with some rare item they'd found, like cast iron pans, or a whole piece of glassware. Usually, families kept those, though. Some of them, like the family in the public room, weren't even buying food because they'd brought their own. She didn't care, as long as things didn't get out of hand. And really, what was she going to do with all the food people gave her? She knew the cook wouldn't mind more pots and pans, though.

Asa was idly watching one of the little girls trying to stay out of the way of the many adult feet. She would flatten herself against the wall, pulling a face as if it too might get stepped on if it were out too far. As Asa smiled at her antics, a drunken young man got out of his seat to take a swipe at someone he'd obviously taken offense to. She closed her eyes for a moment, and the young man slumped back into his chair. She looked at Lis, and the woman hurried over to prop him up before he slid to the floor. She turned again to Asa, and shook her head and grinned. He was totally out. Lis didn't have to ask how Asa did that. She knew.

The usual young men were starting to become loud after drinking more than they were accustomed to. Some of them were making passes at the servers, but Asa knew that Lis could handle them. If the other girls had any real problems, they knew to go to her first. She was great at deflecting them without making them feel like jerks. Unless they *were* jerks. She let them know that, too. Lis and Asa were more friends than employer and employee. Asa trusted her.

It rarely got very bad at times like this. Most of the people in the room were neighbors, or related. You didn't let yourself get *too* out of hand when your aunt or sister might notice.

CHAPTER TWO

Things were starting to change in the room. It was getting late, and tempers were rising along with the amount of cider and beer consumed. There was also less room for each person as more people came in. That made problems all by itself, as elbows bumped and feet were stepped on. There had been more than a couple of times when people reacted and shoved others. Asa could stop the fights before they occurred, but it was wearing on her. It was time to do something about it. Asa called to Lis as she passed, heading over to the family with the little girls.

"Time, Lis. Check out the back room and get anyone who isn't sleeping to leave. I'm moving all the families in there for the night."

Lis hesitated. "Asa, I'll need some help. There are a couple of men back there who aren't going to move easy. I've been ignoring them for a while so you didn't have to take your mind off the crowd. As long as they didn't start anything with anyone else, I figured they'd keep."

Asa frowned. "What do you mean, Lis? What exactly are they doing?"

Lis hesitated again. "Well, you know the family with the little girls? They tried to go back there when they came in. I heard the men tell them it was a private room. I told the family that wasn't true, but they said they would just as soon stay out here. Probably didn't want to cause a problem. I was so busy right then that I forgot about them until now. As far as I've noticed, nobody else has tried to go back there, so I just ignored them."

Asa's eyes flashed in anger. "Well, I think," she said, with a deadly smile, "that those men are about to have company who will make them wish they'd invited the family and a lot of others in."

She headed toward the door.

Lis grinned. "May I watch?" She was one of a very few people who knew what Asa could do.

"Sure. I just wish you'd told me sooner."

As she opened the door to the other room, a gruff voice snarled, "Get out! This is a private room!"

She smiled at the two men, who were sitting at a table playing cards. It wasn't a pleasant expression. Neither of them had even bothered to turn to look at who was at the door.

"Gentlemen, and I use that term loosely, this is *not* a private room."

Asa spoke quietly and calmly. "As a matter of fact, it is being turned over to the families with children, so please gather your things and move out...now."

The larger of the two got up and turned with a sneer on his face.

"And exactly who do you think is gonna make us?"

He looked her up and down. It didn't seem like she'd be much of a problem. Brown hair, gray eyes, short, and rather slightly built. Obviously, they weren't from nearby. No one who knew the inn or any of the people around here would have spoken to Asa like that.

Not even if they hadn't personally learned what she was capable of. People talked, and most knew or had heard of someone who'd tried to cause trouble here. People who misbehaved at the inn learned fast—and they learned hard sometimes. She had already decided that this man was going to learn hard. His friend hadn't said anything, just watched. Maybe he'd be smarter.

She held the door and waved her hand at it as if he hadn't spoken. It was his last chance to get out without trouble. He stepped forward as if to walk through the door and grabbed at her arm to shove her out through it.

He found himself lying on the floor about ten feet from the door. Asa was standing right where she'd been, still holding the door. He started to get up and flinched as his arm gave out under him. His eyes widened, and he looked confused. He tried again, and held the one arm close to him as he rose. He groaned as he inspected it. The wrist was broken.

The other man had been quietly gathering their things.

"Sorry, miss," he apologized. "We'll be leaving right away. My friend here didn't know what he was doing." He gave the other a wry grin. "We're from the other end of the valley."

"Friend?" Asa snorted. "Why didn't you warn him if he's your friend?"

"Well," he started, glancing at the speechless man, who was cradling the wrist to his chest, "I did. I tried to tell him not to do those things, 'cause it would get him a lot of grief. He told me that he wasn't worried about some little woman. I'd heard things about you and said that not all women were the same, and he laughed. He never listens to me. So, I figured seeing is believing."

He smiled sheepishly. "Only worry I had was that you'd knock us both out and I wouldn't have a chance to see him learn."

The other man had stood there without saying a word. His face had become angrier as he listened to the other man talk.

Finally he burst out, "You fool! She could have killed me! I never even knew what hit me until I tried to get off the floor. What are you, crazy?"

"Enough!" Asa waved at the door again. "Get out. Stop in the kitchen. Cayla is our healer. She'll fix the wrist. I don't want to see either of you around here anymore. We have enough trouble as it is, with so many people here. We don't need you. Go wherever you like, just not here. If I see either of you anywhere near here, you'll wish I hadn't."

"But," the troublemaker whined, "where can we go?"

"You should have thought of that before. Go sleep in the woods, for all I care! Out!"

Asa's eyes narrowed as she spoke. The men hurried through the door and back toward the kitchen.

"Start the families coming in, Lis. Make sure each of them has enough room before you let more in."

"If you see either of them in here again, tell me immediately. Warn the others to watch for them. Maybe they will be smart enough to stay away, but being idiots, that isn't likely. And unless they slog through a few miles of water to the other end of the valley, I figure they won't go far." She sighed.

She headed back out to watch the rest of the inn.

·

CHAPTER THREE

Asa was back at the bar, pouring mugs of cider for the servers to hand out when Tom came in. Tom didn't actually work for Asa, but the inn was his base of operations. When she needed a favor, she asked Tom. When someone was looking for a guide or help of some kind, she sent them to Tom. It was a good arrangement.

"It's getting worse," he said, nodding at the offer of cider. "Anyone without a boat probably isn't going to make it here after today unless they know how to swim. I passed a family about two miles down the road that was heading here. Both parents were carrying a little one on their shoulders. The father also had one in his arms. There're spots out there that are as deep as your thighs. I'm wondering if you might take a boat out with me to check around and make sure there aren't any people already stuck? I could go alone, but with you along it'll be a lot quicker."

"Mother, Tom," Asa sighed. "I don't know. This place is

mobbed, and it's getting late. Lis can handle most things that come up, but we've had problems already. Do you think it can wait until tomorrow? By then, I'll know exactly what I've got here. And I'd like to go out. A few hours of silence would be great. So, tomorrow morning?"

"That'll be fine. I don't think it'll get that much worse by then. It's just slowly getting higher and higher. Don't know how much more melt will come from the mountains. That's another thing I'd like to check on." He paused, then sighed. "Well, let's take care of one thing before we start worrying about another. I'll get everything ready for morning. If you need me, I'll be in the stable. Only quiet place around now." He shook his head and got up to leave.

"See you in the morning. It'll be a rest for me." She laughed, and started to turn away…

CHAPTER FOUR

A man came in. He was young, maybe eighteen. He looked around like he was totally lost. Nobody who lived in the valley wore anything but serviceable clothing, but it was clean, for the most part, and well taken care of. Making your own tended to make you careful about what you used. This man looked like he hadn't been decently clothed for a very long time, and it looked like he'd been in a fight or something, with a few rips down one side of his shirt. He walked to the bar, and looking down, he hoarsely asked, "Cider, please?"

Tom looked him up and down and said, "Looks to me like you need more than that."

The man glanced at him quickly, and then slowly drank the mug of cider Asa put on the counter in front of him. He nodded once but kept sipping, looking down.

Tom thought he'd seen a flash of yellow from the man's eyes and stared at him carefully. He'd only seen something like that once before—when Asa had arrived.

"Name's Tom. Don't think I've seen you before. Where did you come into the valley? Not often outsiders find their way here." Nobody had, not since Asa.

The man kept sipping his cider. "Was being chased by a bear, and I slipped and fell, up on the mountain. Couldn't find a way back up and got lost. Just started walking, and here I am. Where is *here*, by the way?"

Tom answered, "Doesn't really have a name. Might have once, but we just call it the valley. And it's big enough that it might have had more than one town. Where you came from, did it have a name?"

Asa had been watching the young man and said to Tom, "He's telling the truth."

At that, the man looked into Asa's face, glimpsed the flash in her eyes, and backed up. Obviously, he'd met someone like her before, and it hadn't been a good experience. "I'm not here to cause any trouble, just had no idea where I was. I'll leave."

Asa quietly said, "If you aren't causing any problems, you don't have to. So, how long have you been traveling alone? Or are you? Alone, I mean."

"I've been traveling alone for quite a while," he said. "The group I was with last year got into a fight, about... Anyway, two of them died, including our, um...leader. There were only five of us to start with, and the other two were a couple. We didn't know each other well. They decided to take off on their own."

"Well, go on into the kitchen and tell Cayla I said to feed you. As long as you aren't here to make a problem, I can probably find some work for you if you want it. At least for a while. Water is going to get pretty deep soon, just so you know. It will make it very hard for you to leave anyway."

She just kept wiping the counter, not engaging him in a staring contest for the moment.

He nodded, smiled shyly, and said, "Appreciate it. I'll do any work you have. By the way, name is Zack." He headed to the kitchen.

"You sure about this?" Tom asked after Zack had walked away. "There is something real different about that boy."

Asa answered in a low voice, "Yes. He isn't here to cause trouble. And by the way," she grinned, "he can hear you even that far away. See you in the morning."

CHAPTER FIVE

"I don't know about leaving that guy here while we are gone. I know you said he was okay, but you just met him, and there is something weird about him that I can't figure out," Tom told Asa as they loaded up the dinghy.

"I talked to him before I came out. He's okay, just lost in more ways than one," she answered.

"Look, I've never questioned you about what you are, and most people just think you are really good at some kind of defense thing and are really smart, but I know you aren't like the rest of us. Neither is he. Why?" Tom never looked up, just started pushing the boat toward the water. He didn't sound confrontational, just curious.

"There were other people like me back where I came from."

She paused for a few seconds, trying to think how to make him understand a world that wasn't like the one here in the valley. It was totally closed off from elsewhere, and the only way in was by accident—the way both she and this new guy had gotten here.

"Some of them aren't very nice. Sometimes power makes people do crazy things. Try to run other's lives, use them for their benefit, make themselves look better—from their own point of view anyway.

"I don't know why I can do what I do. One of the women in the town I come from was using other people to make herself into some kind of boss. Everyone thought she was wonderful. I didn't. People are just people. Some good, some not. Some of them will follow anyone who makes life easier for them, or if it looks like they will.

"Anyway, this woman started out helping others, and soon she was telling them how to do things. Then she was demanding they do things her way. I tend to ask why rather than follow someone blindly. Most of the other people in the town didn't have whatever both she and I have, or at least not as strong. I decided to get away before I ended up in the middle of a fight because I didn't appreciate what she was doing. As I said, a lot of people liked having someone else make their decisions for them. Not me. I left.

"I wandered for some time, and rarely saw any other people. Did pass one town, but at the main road, there were men with guns. Had no interest in even going near that one. Might have just been a good place that guarded their homes, but with what I am, even that could have been a problem.

"Probably wouldn't have gotten here, but as I was heading over the mountain, I hit the place where the big rock slide is and ended up at the bottom.

"Since I've been in the valley, I haven't seen anywhere it would be easy to get out. You know that a few who have tried never came back. No clue if they died or found a way out. Makes it nice here. We rarely get bullies. Not really much here for people who want to take over. People are spread way too far apart. People here just live their lives.

"This guy that showed up last night, he was with a small group of people like him. Two boss-types ended each other, and the others left, probably to search for another group, because those people usually like to be with others of their kind. Another case of people being happier when someone gives them some kind of direction. When they left him, he got lost and ended up here. He might have ended up someone's follower back out there because he isn't the type to try to take over, but because he is here, he might have a decent life. Lonely for the most part without others like him, but he's young and capable. I know how he feels inside, and he feels like a good guy. Give him a chance. The same one you gave me. He is both different from and similar to me. He has something extra like I do, but it made him something else. Different isn't always bad."

She stopped. "Let's get out of here and see what's up out there."

CHAPTER SIX

They spent several hours checking places they hadn't seen someone from at the inn. A few people who were still in their homes said they were doing okay, and thanked them for the checkup. Most other places they checked were empty, until they came to one that had two men trying to pry a door open. Asa sighed and said, "Always have to be a couple of jerks. Let's go take care of them."

The men didn't even notice Asa and Tom coming up to them. Asa went right toward them. They wouldn't be worried about her. Tom slipped around to the other side of the house. As soon as they saw her, they backed off from the door and started talking.

"Uh, we thought we heard someone call for help in there. Is this your place?" She could see on their faces they were going to try something. They hadn't expected to see anyone out here.

When she got closer, she called to them pleasantly, "Hi there. I don't think I know you. Where are you from?" That kept their attention in her direction. Tom quietly came from behind the house, and he didn't waste a second before slamming their heads together. One went down, but the other started to get up, and Tom punched him in the face. Down went the second one.

"*Now* what do we do with them? Can't just leave them here. They will finish what they started." He looked at Asa.

She grinned and said, "You did your part, and now I will do mine."

She knelt and put her hands on each of their heads. She told Tom, "When they wake, they will have memories of something horrible attacking them. They'll get out of the area quickly, scared that it's still near. And they will think twice about coming out to bother people's homes!"

After they finished checking the homes they knew of, they headed to what was normally a small stream to check on the melt. At the moment, it was more like a river. It would be a while before the water level went down. Asa thought, *I just might have to start accepting food from the people coming in.* Hopefully, they wouldn't run out before the water started dropping.

To Tom, she said, "Might have to do another run in a few days. Looks to me like it's going to be quite a while before people can get back to their homes. We'll need a lot more food if that happens. Let me ask around to see who has stored enough stuff at their places that they'd be willing to sell. "

By the time they headed back to the inn, they'd made only one rescue—a momma cat who had dragged her kittens to high ground, only to get stuck on a small island. Momma had jumped right into their boat after Asa called to her, bringing one kitten while Asa went and grabbed the other three. The cat settled down at Asa's feet and stayed calm and quiet, cuddled with her babies.

Tom laughed and said, "That always amazes me, how animals just come to you. Guess the inn has some new family now."

Asa smirked. She wasn't about to add to what he knew and tell him she could talk to them. "Not really. She and her babies belong to a family that's at the inn, although I wouldn't mind keeping one of the kittens." She reached down and ran a finger over one of the furry little heads.

"How do you know this stuff? " Tom just shook his head.

"Same way I knew that guy Zack was okay; I just do. Plus I saw one of the little girls back at the inn in Momma's head!" She grinned.

Tom started thinking back to what he might have thought in Asa's presence and got a little worried. Asa was looking down at the cats, so he didn't see her trying to hold back her grin. She said, "Oh, and the little redhead who just started working for me thinks *you're* cute, too."

Tom's eyes widened, but he looked up with a grin. "Yep, better start watching what I think around you."

CHAPTER SEVEN

They were carrying the dinghy toward the stables when they heard the screaming. They dropped the boat and rushed toward the back of the building. As they turned the corner, they came to a horrible sight. There was some kind of nasty-looking beast standing over a man. Tom pulled out his hunting knife, not that he thought it would take care of this thing. It was huge, not like any regular dog he'd ever seen.

"No, stop, Tom. You don't understand." She held up a hand to stop Tom from coming forward, walked toward the beast, and asked, "What happened?"

"Are you nuts?" yelled Tom. "Get away from that thing!"

It turned and growled, and Tom backed up a little as Asa looked at the man on the ground.

It was the bad-tempered man from last night in the back room, who started yelling, "It's going to kill me! Help me! Make it stop! I-I...came back for something I left, and this *thing* attacked me!"

The beast, which looked more like an overgrown wolf than anything else, turned to the back wall of the inn and sniffed it, growling again. As it turned away, the guy started inching backward, getting as far from it as he could without getting up. The beast spun and went toward him, and he froze.

Asa went over to the wall and smelled something like cooking oil, which soaked a big patch on the corner of the building. Lying on the ground below was a chunk of flint. The guy had been trying to burn her place down. He must have stolen the oil last night when he was in the kitchen. She should have just sent him on his way with the broken wrist.

She stopped and looked around, feeling the area for the guy's friend. She didn't sense him, but it was odd they weren't together.

"Where is your pal?" she snapped at him.

"I don't know, he took off last night," he lied. Asa saw the friend lying on the ground in his mind, either unconscious or dead. It didn't seem to matter which in the man's head. She recognized the area and would go and check on him later, but she didn't think this jerk had it in him to have killed the guy.

Asa snarled, "I should let him kill you right now, but I won't do that to him. If you are ever seen even near here again, I *still* won't let him kill you. I will do it myself. If I hear of you anywhere near here, I will come after you."

She stared into his eyes and let hers flash blue.

He scrambled backward, falling several times as he tried to get away. The beast growled a couple of times, making him move even faster. He turned, looking over his shoulder at the beast, and slid in the mud, falling on his face once but finally getting his feet under him. He was still running when he got out of sight. Between Asa and Zack, she was pretty sure he wouldn't be back, and nobody would believe him if he started talking about them.

As soon as he was out of sight, Asa turned toward the beast and said, "Thank you. Not sure how long it will take, but when you are feeling more yourself, come inside. If you like, I will hire you permanently. If you want to stick around, I mean."

She was pretty sure he'd stay. It was now a place where someone knew what he was and accepted him. That would be hard to find here or anywhere, even if he could find a way out of the valley.

She turned to Tom. "Come on. We have to take the cats to the kitchen. And it will take a while for him to change back."

Asa returned to the dinghy and got the kittens, and, with Momma following her, headed toward the back door.

Tom stood there staring, not quite believing all he'd just seen, and asked, "Zack?"

The beast growled softly, and Asa answered, "Yep. Told you different isn't always bad."

AUTHOR NOTES KAT N. SNOW

I am amazed that I'd ever have a chance to write *Author Notes*. I am thankful to even be included every day in this group of people and read all their ideas and stories.

Michael has gotten together an amazing following by making a world many people want to be a part of. I've read so much science fiction and fantasy in my life, and his is some of the best out there.

None has ever taken me in so many directions while still being connected to the main story or made me care so much about the characters and their lives. So, my thanks to him for showing us this world, and now letting me be part of it.

Kathleen

HAIKU FROM THE KURTHERIAN UNIVERSE

Michael has come back.
All hail the Dark Messiah!
BA just smacks him

———

What are we eating?
Bethany Anne decrees it!
Michael cooks dinner

TREMOR

BY LUCINDA PEBRE

At only sixteen years old, Adaire is an expert in loss. The Dark Society took her family, and now they want the only person she has left.

Adaire is determined to fight for a future. However, to escape her captors and be reunited with her friend Calum, she will need to uncover her dormant magic. Only then will she have a chance to return home.

Set in the world of The Hidden Magic Chronicles by Justin Sloan and Michael Anderle.

To Anna Harland, a fantastic friend who is always there to listen to my crazy ideas, and Marcus Bishop, who loves me as I am.

Thank you to the Kurtherian Fans Write Facebook Group for

their wonderful support, especially in spotting wayward commas and pesky British words. Natalie, Erika and Sarah, you do a great job.

To Michael Anderle and Justin Sloan for creating such an amazing universe and giving us the chance to play.
— Lucinda

CHAPTER ONE

"Calum, quick. Someone's coming."

Adaire held the door ajar. Sweat beaded her hairline. If the guards caught them, the consequences would be dire, but it was more important to honor the pact with her friend—to cause their captors as much trouble as possible.

It was a miracle the kitchen had been empty. Every other time they had tried, there had been at least one servant bustling around.

A teenage boy with red hair and freckles raced toward her, his arms full of pastries. Next time they would have to bring something to carry them in. It was unbelievable that she thought there was going to be another time.

Adaire led them away from the footsteps, in the opposite direction from where they needed to go. With no choice, they ran deeper into the castle.

They raced past colorful tapestries, coats of arms, and a hideous stag's head that watched them from glassy eyes. Torches placed at intervals provided enough light to see where they were going, and their thick smoke curled to hang beneath the ceiling. As they passed, the flames shrank to embers.

Adaire glanced at Calum. "Be careful, else they'll know it was you."

He grinned. "There's no proof."

"Since when do they need proof? You're also leaving them a trail."

Now, instead of dying, the rest burned brighter. Adaire thought. *That's better. Let them use up all the fuel.*

When there wasn't any sound of pursuit, they slowed and turned a corner into a narrow corridor with unadorned stonework. It smelled musty, and there weren't any torches, making the shadows deep.

Adaire stopped and pointed out the footprints they had left in the dust.

Calum shook his head, unable to do anything with arms full of pastries.

Adaire scowled and shrugged out of her coat to trail it after them. "These must be the servant's quarters."

"We'll never find the way out," Calum hissed in her ear.

She noticed that he hadn't discarded the food, despite his conviction that they were lost. Adaire wasn't sure she was *capable* of getting lost. She always had a sense of where she was in the bigger picture.

She ignored a jab in her ribs from Calum's elbow. Something about this section of the wall intrigued her. Nothing appeared different from the rest, but her fingers tingled when she moved them across the stone. The tingling grew stronger or weaker depending on where she placed her hands.

Calum took a bite out of a pastry.

Her stomach made a strange noise and her mouth watered, but this was important. She focused on her fingers, searching for the...seam.

Calum smirked through a mouth full of buttery goodness. His eyes challenged her to resist the stolen cakes.

Ah, there. A grating sound echoed in the corridor and part of the wall swung inwards.

Calum almost dropped his armload as he stumbled back. "Some warning would have been nice."

Voices and hurried footsteps came from the main corridor. It sounded as if they were just around the corner.

Adaire slipped into the narrow space, and Calum squeezed in after. They leaned against the stone to push it back into place. It wasn't heavy. Some sort of mechanism must allow it to open and close.

Adaire strained to hear anything. Whoever was on the other side of the wall might know about their hiding place. The thought must have occurred to Calum because he stopped chewing and his breathing was faster than usual.

Adaire's eyes adjusted. It wasn't totally dark. Light came from small holes set above their heads in the opposite wall.

When nothing happened, she nudged Calum, and they started to move.

"Can't stand cramped spaces," he murmured.

They didn't bother Adaire, not one bit. If she listened carefully, she could hear slight shifts in the stone. When she told Calum, he said she was daft and that everyone knew rock was rock.

"Come on." She took them left, pleased that Calum trusted her to lead.

The passage was so narrow that if she raised her arms a small bit, she could touch both walls. There wasn't enough light to see the floor, and if her toe hadn't landed on the edge of a step, she would have fallen.

"Stairs," she whispered.

He moved closer until he was touching her and could follow her movement. Perhaps he was hoping for a soft landing if he fell.

With her hands on the walls at either side, she felt her way down to the bottom.

The sound of a conversation made her stop. Calum bumped into her back, propelling her forward a few steps. She scowled in his direction.

It took a moment to work out that the voice must have come from a room on the other side of the wall. They moved close to listen. Perhaps the corridor had been built for spying before the fake laird had claimed the castle.

"...too early to tell." The soft voice made the fine hairs on the back of her neck stand up. It was Laird Scott, or Scroat, as the kids called him.

A man with a local accent responded, "Aye, it would be best to keep the poor stock here. Move out those with potential for more specialized training."

"Let it be so."

Adaire grabbed Calum's arm. She was "poor stock," her magic never doing anything no matter what they did to "encourage" it. But Calum's fire magic was the best.

"You may leave," Scroat told the unknown man.

Adaire wanted to see who he was before he left, but the spyholes were too high.

"Right you are." Footsteps moved away.

Calum pushed her with his shoulder. She understood the urgency. Wherever Scroat was, the mystic was never far away, and he would detect their presence.

They continued in the same direction. Stairs took them up and then down at intervals. At one point the corridor branched into two, with one dropping into the earth.

Calum stared into the darkness. "I'm not going that way."

Adaire wondered if the other end of the tunnel went outside the grounds. If she wanted to explore down there, it would have to be without Calum.

They continued in a straight line until cool air indicated that they were approaching an outside wall. The corridor narrowed until it was little more than a crack, which they had to move through sideways.

Adaire bent her leg and cracked her knee on the stone. The pain brought tears to her eyes and made her more careful as she shuffled to the end.

"Thank my hairy arse," Calum exclaimed when they reached a grate where there was room to stand side by side. "I thought if I breathed out, I'd be stuck in there."

"More like there was a chance you might have to leave the cakes." She noted that he had grazed his forearms to keep the armful.

Metal barred their way outside. They stared at it, dreading having to retrace their steps where the odds of getting caught were high. After all, someone had followed them.

"Do you think you can get under?" Calum asked.

She looked at the shallow depression. "You're bigger than me. If you can, I can."

Years of not enough food had made them short and lean.

Calum's eyes slid away. "As long as you get out, I can always go back the way we came."

"No."

"I knew you'd say that." He sighed. "Here, then."

Adaire wasn't hungry anymore, but she took the food. She was tempted to drop it for the rats, but it was for the other children more than them.

Calum peeled off his clothes. She averted her eyes and waited until he wasn't looking to peek. He was skinny, but a coating of muscle gave his body a distinct shape.

"Don't drop them in the mud." He placed the clothes on top of the pastries. "It'll stop you eating the buns."

She stuck out her tongue. The prospect of getting naked was not appealing.

Calum was already on his knees with his white ass sticking up in the air. Like a lizard, he slithered in the damp mud, sliding easily under the grating.

Once he was on the other side, she passed his clothes through, and he dressed.

He took the pastries. "That's lucky. It looks like we're at the back of the building."

He raised his eyebrows in a challenge, but she was no coward.

"Look away, then."

He chuckled but turned his back to her. "Hurry, we don't want to be missed."

Adaire undressed quickly, doing her best to ignore the cold. *Mind over matter.* A stab of unexpected grief hit her in the chest. It was something her da used to say.

"What's wrong?"

Calum had felt the change without her saying a word. She was impressed that he didn't use it as an excuse to look at her body.

"Just remembering da."

He'd understand, having lost everyone too. That was why they named the day the raiders came "The End"—because it had been the end of a normal life, although they'd stopped brooding about it years ago. She reminded herself that it didn't do any good to live in the past.

Adaire slithered under the grate. Once over the shock of cold, she enjoyed the sensation of smooth mud on her body.

She accepted her clothes from Calum. "You better not have sneaked a look at my ass."

By the way his pale skin went bright red, she knew he had.

Dressing over a layer of mud felt wrong, but then much about life was just plain wrong these days.

CHAPTER TWO

The guards called the old cowshed "the barracks" as if that made it something it wasn't. They scrambled through a loose board to get inside.

The straw strewn across the floor made it even more like a cowshed. Adaire felt sorry for the cows that used to live here. In winter the wooden slats let in freezing drafts, and in summer they baked.

There were no lessons today, so the children must have noticed their absence, but even the little ones were careful not to see too much in case they were questioned.

The eight kids were playing a game with stones at the far side of the shed. Only Aila was doing her own thing, drawing with a stick in the dirt.

Calum and Adaire went to adjacent beds. Calum's coat hid the pastries.

"Where are we going to leave the food?" Adaire whispered.

Neither Calum or Adaire wanted to let their captors

know the depth of their hatred for the people who had murdered their clan. Although Calum could stop the mystic from getting into their heads, the bastard could still read those around them. If they gave out the food, the guards would catch them within the day.

Calum juggled the rolls. "You create a distraction, and I'll put the food outside the door."

Adaire smiled. There was nothing wrong with Calum's overall strategy—let the enemy believe they were stupid while thwarting them at every opportunity.

Until they take Calum away. The unwelcome thought was difficult to process, so she ignored it.

"I've got a better idea." She took the food and walked into the middle of the space. "Look what some thieving guard dropped!"

There was a cry of excitement, which Adaire hurriedly shushed. It wouldn't do for a guard to barge in to see what had caused the noise.

Later, Adaire and Calum lay side by side on their straw mattresses to have a private conversation. With their heads close together there was less chance of being overheard.

Calum said, "That was stupid. Now they'll know it was us."

"I think we have bigger things to worry about." She propped herself on one arm. "Calum, they are going to separate us."

At least until now, their captors couldn't see into their hearts. Calum had made sure the mystic experienced darkness when he tried. The pasty-faced-freak never lingered long.

"They've already taken everything else. Now, you won't be able to protect my mind. " Adaire didn't mention how much she was going to miss him, because that was too hard.

She rubbed her eyes, angry at being weak. Loss should have become easier with practice, but it hadn't worked that way.

Calum shook his head. "I've been thinking about this. Protection doesn't stop when we're out of sight of each other." He rolled over to face her. "It's possible that distance doesn't make any difference."

That was true. Calum had become so good that it took no effort for him to confuse the mystic.

He pushed up to sit on the edge of the bed. "If I can do it, so can you. It's a learned skill rather than something I was born with."

Adaire wasn't sure. She didn't have any valuable skills.

"Do you remember the first time I did it?" Calum asked.

She nodded, seeing Imogen's terror again at not being able to spread the fire. Imogen was too young for her magic to be consistent, but their captors could be cruel.

"I did it out of necessity, to protect Imogen from the mystic," Calum explained.

"I understand what you are saying, but…"

"No buts, Adaire. You have to do this."

"Okay, but since there's no way to test your theory until it happens," she sat up, "I'm going to help the little ones get ready for bed."

Calum shook his head. "It's risky this early. He might be around."

She gave him a look over her shoulder. "I know, but what isn't risky?"

He started to get up. "I'll go."

"No, I won't let him take anything else from me." She could see by the look on Calum's face that he was afraid for her.

Before they could set off for the river that served as their washroom, rain began to drum on the roof. Adaire shared a look with Calum. There was little chance Scroat would risk getting his perfumed curls wet.

Two girls and a boy were small enough to need help. They still cried for their mothers at night, so the earlier they were asleep, the better.

It was funny how just when she was feeling sorry for herself, she was reminded there were people worse off.

As Water Clan, Edan and Aila's spirits were bound to show up to cause mischief at the river. Since Leanna's was wind, hers was likely to join in as well. Adaire didn't care. It was nice to see the children forget for a short time.

Adaire used to have a spirit, indicating that she would develop magic when she was older. It was the only reason she hadn't died with the rest of the clan. Since she came from a fire clan, everyone presumed she would develop fire magic, but it had never happened.

There were times Adaire had tried to hide her spirit because it wasn't like the others. Rather than light and golden, it was a drab, dark creature with enormous owl-like eyes. Also, instead of flying, both its feet were firmly stuck to the ground, and it never showed any affinity for fire.

At the time it hadn't mattered what it looked like, because everyone knew spirits weren't real. They were a promise of the magic to come. But later, when her fire magic never materialized, she wondered if there was something wrong with her.

Nothing Scroat had done made any difference. Fire burned her flesh as if she had no magic at all.

Calum said her magic would come in its own time, but it never had. Now, at sixteen, she was too old to hope.

For whatever reason, their captors only wanted children who were going to develop magic, which was why they had murdered her baby brother. He'd been too young to have developed a spirit when the raiders came. In some ways she was lucky Scroat took an interest, else she'd have been killed before now.

Adaire remembered how he had studied her until it made her squirm. "Whoever would have thought nature could have produced white-blonde hair with hazel eyes, hey, Troy?"

"Yes, Laird."

She'd only been ten years old but had known not to cry in front of him. It had been the first time she'd thought of herself as different.

"She has a spirit, so her magic will come out." He waved his hand in Adaire's direction. "She stays."

Just like that, she'd been allowed to live.

CHAPTER THREE

The guards came at dawn to take Calum along with six other children.

"Stay alive, and stay away from him," Calum whispered. "I will find a way to get in touch."

Children were expendable in this place, so they both knew it'd do no good to fight.

For the first time in three years, Adaire hadn't been able to stop the tears. She stared after the wagon until Troy, one of the guards, took her arm and pulled her away.

She struggled, but it was weak and half-hearted.

He gave her a serious look. "Stop that, or the others will expect me to clout you."

Curiosity penetrated her despair, and she stopped. "Why wouldn't you just do it?"

"I should." He screwed his face into a vicious mask.

He wasn't serious. Adaire knew because she'd become a master at reading other people's intentions.

"Things will get better if you stop fighting," he told her.

"Was that what you did?"

Troy considered the question. "Could be."

"You don't sound like the others."

He scratched his beard. "Ah, it's true, I'm not from these parts." He looked across the river as if his home were on the far side. "My people came to your land for reasons you wouldn't like."

Even with his shaved head, it wouldn't have occurred to her what he was if the other guards hadn't complained about him.

"They call you 'Barskall.'"

"It's true. Where I come from, we eat children."

"That's a lie," she said with more conviction than she felt. "That'd make you no better than *him*." She looked at Scroat, who was surveying the tearful children from a balcony.

When Scroat's eyes caught hers, they lingered too long.

Troy glanced at Laird Scott. "You want to watch yourself there."

She balled her hands into fists. "Tell me how I can do that, exactly?"

He shrugged and scratched his beard again. She couldn't see the point of facial hair if it itched so much.

"Come on. I'm to take you to the barracks."

The last three children and Adaire stayed in the shed for the rest of the day. When the daily rations came, she let the others eat her share while she laid on the mattress and counted spiders' webs. Adaire wondered if it were possible to die from numbness. Eventually, she fell asleep.

She dreamt she was home, just outside the village. Morning light glinted off waves to her right, while the loch on her left was as still as glass. Gentle green slopes rose to dramatic jagged rocks above. It was more beautiful than she remembered, but she wasn't interested in the view. Calum sat at the edge of the loch.

He climbed to his feet. "Finally! I've been waiting for ages."

"Is this real?"

He spun in a circle, arms wide. "It looks real to me."

She ran to him and punched his arm.

"Ow, that hurt."

"It's a dream, how can it hurt?"

He gave her a real smile, showing two dimples, one on either cheek. Before The End, he'd had a three-dimple smile, the third on his chin. For now, she'd settle for two.

He grabbed her hand, pulling her down to sit with him. "I think we're in my head."

She laughed. "I'm not sure how I feel about that."

From the edge of the loch, they watched a golden eagle hunt at the base of the mountain.

"Where did they take you?" she asked.

"They split us up. All those with fire are a day's ride away. I don't know where the others went." The intensity of the fire on his right increased. "You know how many bloody castles there are here in Roneland."

He took off his shoes to dangle his feet in the freezing water. "They managed to find one that's not much more than a ruin, the nutjackers."

She took his hand. "This is great—more than I could have hoped for—but I need to see you for real."

He pulled her close. "Too right. Let's make a new pact: to go home together."

CHAPTER FOUR

In the morning, Adaire attended lessons with the other children. Then, while they practiced magic, she cleaned the shed.

Tomorrow she would be expected to clean in the castle, and Scroat would go out of his way to find her. He hadn't done anything yet, and she made sure not to encourage him, but he gave her things. Lovely-smelling soap, a flower, and once, a pair of shoes. Afterward, she would throw the gift in the river.

One of the guards saw her last time. "Ungrateful whelp."

Fortunately, Troy had been on patrol. "Leave the girl alone."

"What do you care, Barskall?"

The mystic watched from the castle porch. He was too far away to hear, but she could tell by the way he looked at her that he couldn't see into her head. Calum had been right.

She'd run back to the shed, afraid the guard would tell Scroat what she'd done. After that, she'd worked even harder at avoiding him. She must have been successful because he ordered Troy to fetch her.

Troy's footsteps were heavy. "Sorry, but you understand that I have to take you to him."

It was weird how her mind refused to leave the work she had yet to complete, as if it mattered. But she put down the brush she'd just used to clean the fireplace and followed him to Scroat's study.

He was by the window when they entered the room. Adaire knew she was in trouble, because whatever he wanted, she would not be willing to give it.

He looked at her as he said, "You may leave, Troy."

Adaire made sure to stand tall. "What can I do for you?"

"There's no need for formality."

Adaire thought that formality was the only feeble thing she had to protect her.

Scroat stepped into her space. "Call me Dale."

She crossed her arms. "I'd rather not, Laird Scott."

He was too close, smelling of the roses he kept in a big vase in the dining room. It wasn't a bad scent, but it was somehow wrong.

He studied her face. "Bones as fine and delicate as a bird."

Adaire dropped her eyes. Not out of respect, but to hide the fury there.

With one finger, he lifted her chin. "I could make life easier for you if you'd be nice to me."

The thought of lying with the man who had murdered her family made her feel sick. She backed away.

Who would help her? Not even Troy would be able to do anything to stop him. The room had taken on a surreal aspect, as if she weren't there. Something rumbled below the castle.

"Don't be afraid. I'm not going to force you." He moved to the fireplace. "But without magic, you are of little use. Think about it."

Adaire ran to the kitchen, which was empty. The servants had probably been sent elsewhere. She stole a sharp knife and hacked off her hair.

The cook found her rocking in front of the fire. The old woman had gently removed the knife from her stiff fingers and swept up the white-blonde strands.

The next day was bright and warm, with the promise of growth and new life. Adaire wondered what Calum was doing. The guards stared longer than usual, but nobody asked her what had happened to her hair. They probably knew.

She almost charged straight into Scroat, who had been waiting outside the shed. He reached for her, and even though she told her body to be still, she couldn't help flinching.

"So nervous, little bird." He cupped her cheek with a smooth hand. "You try to make yourself ugly. It just intrigues me more."

Troy's voice came from over his shoulder. "Laird, there's a visitor at the gate. Says you're expecting him. He's on the goddess' business."

Scroat whipped around and, with a glare at Troy, marched off.

"Thank you." The relief made her legs weak.

"What for?"

She would go along with the pretense that he hadn't saved her on purpose.

Troy leaned on a spear, scanning the grounds. "Sometimes it's easier not to fight the inevitable."

"Is that what you do?"

"I suppose."

He was as much a slave as her.

"I want to go home," she said, rubbing burning eyes.

Troy let out a heavy sigh. "Yes, it's strange how we don't appreciate home until it's gone."

A guard appeared from around the corner of the shed and Troy moved off.

Adaire walked to the castle, hoping Scroat would stay busy with his visitor. Talking to Troy had made her aware of how alone she was. If she hadn't had Calum in her dreams, she'd go mad.

It was time she made plans to leave. She hadn't been able to come up with a plan that involved taking the three young children, but, she could explore the tunnels under the castle in preparation for escape.

Adaire spent the next day working in the kitchens. The cook, who everyone called "Cook," gave her a bowl of venison stew.

"Yee're too thin, child."

Adaire forgave her for calling her a child when she tasted the stew. She'd never tasted anything so glorious in her life.

She mopped the bowl with a chunk of fresh bread. "Why have you got separate pots?"

"Ah, that's for his Lairdship." She lowered her voice. "Never touch that pot."

Adaire nodded, stuffing the bread in her mouth.

"We be sure to spit in it to show our appreciation." She winked.

Adaire almost choked with laughter.

CHAPTER FIVE

How annoying that the anticipation of seeing Calum delayed her getting to sleep.

When she arrived it was early evening, with the sun dropping toward the horizon. The smell of grass took her back to another time. Alone in their usual spot, she pushed her fingers into the earth. Moist soil caught under her fingernails.

She closed her eyes to hear her brother splashing in the water and her mother's complaint that he was part fish.

Calum flopped down beside her and started a small fire.

She rubbed her eyes and leaned into him, soaking up his dependable warmth. "I thought you needed fire to use fire magic?"

He grinned. "Not here." Then he became serious. "What happened to your hair?"

"It was annoying me."

Calum's brow furrowed, giving the impression he was

about to ask more, but he shook his head. "There's talk of us attacking the clans."

Adaire shivered, even though the fire was warm and it was never cold in their dream world. "Like what they did to our clan?"

Calum poked the fire with a finger and flames curled around his arm as if seeking contact. "When they raided our clan, I think they wanted children. Us—"

She finished his sentence, "To train as weapons against our people."

"I need to get away, Adaire. I can't... I just can't." Calum stopped speaking, unable to say anymore.

Adaire shuffled until she was virtually in his lap. "Okay, then, what are the options?"

"I've thought about it." He grabbed her arm. "Because they're all fire mages, they never watch us near the sea, and you know I'm a good swimmer."

The image of her brother playing in the loch came back. She didn't even know if it was a real memory. Her heart hurt; what if Calum drowned? She would be alone forever.

He squeezed her. "It's risky, but we're barely surviving. This isn't life, and if there's a chance to escape..."

She wasn't sure that throwing away what she had was the answer. Life had taught her to grasp what she could and appreciate the hell out of it.

CHAPTER SIX

It was late the next day when Adaire was called to see Scroat. She felt dizzy and wondered if she was ill. If so, she would make every effort to infect him.

He was behind the big oak desk in his study. "I have sad news. The boy you knew..."

Adaire didn't hear anything else. "Knew" was the worst word in existence. If she could eradicate one word, it would be that one.

Scroat shuffled papers on his desk. "Perhaps you will reconsider my offer."

Was he going to do this now?

A scream was building. "Can I go?"

"Of course."

He was lying. Adaire didn't feel any different, and she would if Calum was dead. If she could get to sleep, he would be waiting for her.

The dizziness was worse when she closed her eyes, and

the more she wanted to sleep, the longer it took. Her face was wet, but eventually, she slept.

On waking in the cowshed, her mind full of images and shadows, all she knew was that she hadn't been home. Was it lost to her forever, or had worry stopped her?

The shed was too quiet. The children were asleep, and when she climbed through the loose board, there were no guards. Perhaps they'd given up watching them.

Dawn was a faint line over the forest. It would soon be light, and there was no point waiting. At the back of her mind, Adaire knew it would be better to plan, but all she could think was that if she couldn't go home in her dreams, she had to get there somehow.

The dizziness was still there, but manageable. Adaire had no food or provisions, no weapons, and no plan. Nothing mattered except getting home.

Without returning for anything, Adaire raced to the grate. She was in too much of a hurry to remove her clothes, not caring about mud. With lots of tugging and ripping, she was through. She regretted not having explored the tunnels earlier.

She shuffled sideways through the crack, and once it widened into a corridor, she ran. Crashing down the steps, she avoided spraining an ankle by holding onto the walls.

Angry voices came from one of the rooms. Adaire had an awful feeling that someone had already discovered her absence. She should have left her clothes next to the river, so they thought she'd killed herself.

The corridor divided, and without pause, she slipped and slid down a steep slope. The walls became damp and slick with green moss. There was no light at all. Adaire had visions of plummeting over a cliff or running smack into a wall, but she didn't dare slow down.

If she'd escaped late at night, it would have been less likely that someone would notice her gone this soon. Thoughts flitted through her head, but they didn't slow her down.

The ground leveled out, and she found herself running through ankle-deep water. What if the tunnel came out in the castle grounds? Then she'd be stuck forever...or until she agreed to be Scroat's mistress. She'd rather die.

Ahead a patch of light grew until she was at the entrance to the tunnel. She had no idea how far she had run. Her eyes adjusted to the brilliance of day.

Clouds covered the sun, but she could see that it was halfway to its pinnacle, making it midmorning. Too much time had passed. There was a real danger that the search had expanded beyond the castle and grounds.

Her hands were bright red like they were in her nightmares. It took her a moment to realize she'd scraped them on the walls.

Like a bird let out of its cage, she wasted precious time staring at the forest. This was the nearest she'd come to freedom since they'd brought her to the prison as a ten-year-old.

CHAPTER SEVEN

They were waiting in the beautiful forest. The bright green of it was almost too much for her senses.

She was surprised that so many had bothered to chase her. Later she would think that they couldn't afford to give up. Not because she was valuable, but because they didn't want any information to reach the clans.

She had no strategy, and couldn't think clearly with adrenaline pounding through her veins.

Her sodden feet hit old leaves and mulch as she leaped over branches and darted through trees. Brambles snatched at her legs, leaving bloody scratches even through her clothes. Each breath was a loud rasp in her head.

Something crashed through the foliage, and men shouted to each other. The birds had gone quiet. Only Adaire was out in the open, wishing she could hide with the forest creatures. This close to freedom, she would rather die than go back.

The sound of breaking branches and crashing was so loud, it sounded as if they were on top of her.

Then she saw the determined faces of the hated guards, out for blood. Her brain could not process their words, but she picked up on their pleasure at being so close to catching her. The nearest guard was a few feet away and had a crazed smile on his ugly face.

Adaire stopped in a clearing, her chest heaving. The desire to run and hide had gone, replaced by a sense of injustice. It consumed her until something snapped. A surge of strength forced its way out of her small body, and the ground shook as if there were an earthquake.

The guard slowed, looking around as if expecting to find the cause of the shaking. His confused expression was the last thing she saw before something sucked him beneath the ground.

A muffled cry came from the soil and rocks where he had been moments before. Adaire couldn't believe what she'd done. There were too many, but by God, she'd take as many out as she could.

"Who's next?" she shouted to the remaining five men, who were staring around in confusion.

Two went under in a cloud of dust before they knew what was happening. The others ran in circles, not wanting to present an easy target.

A wave of tiredness hit Adaire, but she couldn't stop. They belonged under the ground where they couldn't cause more harm.

The earth sucked more under, but darkness had started to creep in at the edges of her vision.

The sound of more guards crashing through the forest was the last thing she knew before she succumbed to darkness.

CHAPTER EIGHT

Adaire served a sentence for her escape attempt in the place where they questioned the children. Not that she cared.

Images haunted her. Bright blood, much brighter than it should have been, leaking from the wound in her mother's neck. The broken body of her baby brother tossed into the bushes. All was accompanied by the shouts and screams of people she knew and loved.

The mystic visited to tell her that she'd killed four guards. One they had managed to dig out before he suffocated.

Had she killed Troy? She couldn't remember the faces of those she'd buried.

Did they expect her to feel bad? She couldn't pretend remorse, except perhaps for Troy. They told her she'd go mad, and that she deserved it. Perhaps she already was.

It was weird, how grief insulated her from the terror of

being trapped again. She certainly used it against the mystic at every opportunity.

He explained slowly and carefully, so she would understand that she had earth magic. As if she hadn't been able to work that out for herself. She only recognized the trap when he took that information from her mind.

Adaire wondered whether she could break through the stone floor. Not that she would try, because she suspected that they left her here alone to attempt to escape again. It was their way of finding out about her skills. She'd never been stupid, though.

Curled in on herself, she thought about Calum. With him dead, there was no reason to go on, except for revenge. She had the means. That way, she could make her life count for something.

The clang of the outer door signaled the return of the mystic. It didn't matter. There was no fight left in her, or at least that was what she repeated over and over in her mind.

She felt the pressure as he entered her mind, and clenched her teeth. Her body shook as she fought for control, trying not to hurt him like she was being hurt. Instead, she focused on memories of death and grief in all its vividness. She protected her inner self, while she trusted her subconscious to plan.

Let them see the broken parts. Pretend to go along with them so that she could get out. Troy had been right; there was no fighting them.

The mystic didn't stay long, his nose wrinkling at the stench. Strange how it didn't offend her anymore. He nodded at the guard as he left. After he'd gone the scent of roses lingered, but that could have been a nightmare.

"Move, girl." The guard jabbed with the blunt end of his spear, catching her shoulder.

The dull pain barely registered, and she struggled to stand. She was able to use the wall on her right to balance, but on taking a step, she swayed. The guard cursed and grabbed her arm, almost yanking her shoulder out of the socket to prevent her from falling to the dirty floor.

Every muscle in her body screamed and tears came to her eyes, but she staggered out of the place.

It took a week until she recovered enough to start training. She didn't hide her magic and tried hard to succeed at tasks.

The last of the children were gone. She was alone, except for guards who hated and feared her for killing their colleagues. Scroat stayed away, and she wondered if it were a strategy to make her feel desperate and isolated enough to fall into his bed.

Part of her wanted them to know they were going to die. To explain how taking away the children was their biggest mistake. If they'd kept the children she would have had to protect them, but now all she had to do was focus on making them pay.

The mystic visited from time to time, scanning her mind and forcing her to lie. In some ways, he was worse than Scroat.

Adaire showed him what he wanted to see. She used the tricks she'd learned from Calum to convince him that what he saw on the surface was everything. Inside was a different story. Deep in her heart, she only cared about going home one last time. That need hadn't dimmed.

She didn't plan beyond getting there and didn't worry

about being captured. By the time she'd finished, there wouldn't be anyone to chase her.

"Are you making up for lost time?" she asked the mystic.

"Careful, peasant, that sounds like dissent."

She could have shown him true dissent but held back. Deep below, the earth shifted. That happened a lot now, and she had to fight to stay in control.

In sleep, she was afraid of going home and being there alone. Instead, she retreated to the dark earth, where the soil and rocks shifted.

The next day, Troy was in the yard. She was glad that he hadn't died.

He made a raspy sound, his version of laughter. "I see you, girl."

Perhaps he did. If so, he was the only one. He led her to the field to train for the last time. Afterward, she saw him in the distance, relieving the gate guard.

Scroat chose that day to watch. His eyes burned into her as she moved soil and rocks into shapes. Satisfied that his fascination with her had not dimmed, she continued to perfect her technique.

The rough plan in her head had started to acquire details, and she needed to convince Scroat that she wouldn't hurt him.

A few days later he called her to the castle, asking to see her before he left on some mission. She had tried to wash off some of the dirt that was ingrained in her skin before the meeting.

At the entrance, the mystic stood aside to let her pass. There was nothing of interest to him in her mind. Since

Calum had died, she'd appeared to be an open book, and that was okay.

"The laird would like privacy for this meeting," she told him.

He sneered, believing he knew the reason. "Leave that here." He indicated the bag on her shoulder.

She shrugged and dropped it to the ground. There was nothing she couldn't do without, just food and clothes. There'd been more of both since her magic had appeared.

A guard led her to the familiar study, where Scroat stood at ease next to the window. He was more relaxed than she'd ever seen him, dressed in black cotton pants and a robe, opened to reveal his naked chest. She stared at the light dusting of fine hairs on his torso.

He smiled, and when she lifted her eyes, he took both hands. "I've missed you, little bird."

She returned his smile and held onto him without speaking, not trusting the right words to come out.

"It is good that you've come around to our way of thinking. You will be an asset to the goddess' cause."

She lowered her eyes. "Is that why you asked to see me?"

He brought her left hand to his lips, closed his eyes, and kissed her knuckles. Revulsion washed over her, and she was thankful the mystic was not near.

She prepared for when he opened his eyes, but the pleasant smile plastered on her face must not have been convincing because he abruptly dropped her hands.

His tone had changed. "I have a job for you." He moved to his desk to pick up a piece of paper. "Think of it as a test."

Adaire nodded as if she weren't screaming inside. *Nothing matters.*

"I don't need to tell you what will happen if you fail."

"Dale, I'd like to thank you."

That look was back in his eyes—the one she suspected meant he was thinking about sex.

He came toward her. "Do you now see the benefits of a relationship with me?"

This might be her only chance.

"It isn't that. I'm just so grateful." She smiled

His face softened. "I think we should start again."

She stepped in close and slid the kitchen knife up through his abdomen into his diaphragm. "You really shouldn't leave knives lying around."

The shock in his eyes was almost worth everything. He hadn't thought Adaire was capable.

Warm blood flowed over her hands as Scroat repeatedly swallowed, making a rasping noise in his throat. His whole body was tense and heavy . With the knife still in her hand, she let him slide to the floor.

"I could have let you die with the rest, but it felt too impersonal."

With that, she dropped the blade. She wiped her hands on the drapes, unable to do anything about the blood on her clothes, although the black material only appeared wet.

By the time she'd finished, Scroat had stopped breathing. He lay in the center of a puddle of bright red blood.

"Goodbye, Scroat."

She walked to the front door as if she had every right to be there. Grabbing her bag from the porch, she slung it over her shoulder.

Then she detoured to the kitchen, where the servants were preparing the midday meal with one less knife. "There's a fire in the study. Everyone needs to leave."

Adaire didn't wait to see if they listened; it was the only warning she could afford. Halfway across the yard, she reached into the earth beneath the castle.

The ground shook as a chasm opened and the building folded into it. A cloud of dust billowed into the air, and shouts of alarm were lost in the crash of masonry.

Troy was at the gate, staring at the mound of rubble. "Now, that was impressive."

The mystic stepped into view, his face contorted. "What have you done?"

Adaire concentrated on the ground. Before she could do anything, a sword punched through his chest. The mystic stared down at the blade. As blood soaked into his clothing, he crumpled to his knees.

It took a moment for her brain to catch up to what had happened. She lifted her head from the mystic.

"I hope you find what you're looking for." Troy smiled, stepping over the mystic's body.

"You were right; things got better when I stopped fighting." She stepped through the gate to freedom. "Time to go home."

CHAPTER NINE

The Dark Society might catch her eventually but not until she returned home a final time. Afterward, she would be ready to die and join Calum in heaven or hell.

The journey across wild terrain was long, but Adaire strode onward with a single purpose.

When she reached the road leading to the summer isles, a landslide blocked the way. Adaire coaxed the rocks and earth to part long enough to let her through. She was tired, but being so close to their place kept her going. She had no thought about what would happen once she reached her destination.

Nothing matters.

She'd run out of food two days ago. Once she got to where she needed to be, she could sleep and dream of Calum.

Beyond the landslide, it was easy going. There was a cracked and broken road to follow, with small lochs to the left and mountains on the right.

She didn't stop to watch a pair of ospreys hunt over the clear water or the stag that stood meters away. His nose sniffed the air before he turned and moved into the trees.

The road took her to the place she'd only visited in dreams for the last six years. It hadn't changed.

Her eyes were blurry, and at first, she thought the little shape on the bank of the loch was another deer. Then it stood, unmistakably human.

Her heart banged against her ribcage. What if it was one of them who had come to take her back?

Then she saw a flickering fire, and the figure started toward her. Something about him was familiar, but she dared not believe. If it weren't him, she wouldn't survive the second loss.

"Calum?"

Despite her exhaustion, she started to run. The bag fell from her shoulder, bouncing in the dust on the road.

It might be a dream or a ghost, but she didn't care as long as he was here with her. Now, she couldn't see for tears, but firm and very real arms came about her, tight as a vice. She cried into Calum's chest. The smoky smell of him was real. When she could see again, he was the same as in her dreams, except tired and maybe a little older.

"I thought you were dead," he said into her hair.

"They told me *you'd* died." Her words were an accusation.

"I know. I'm sorry." He pulled back to look at her face. "I almost drowned when a wave took me out to sea. It was bad. I swallowed more water than a fish and couldn't swim any farther."

She traced his face with her hands.

"The sea spat me out. I woke up on a beach, sunburned to a crisp." He turned his head, so she could see that one side of his face was darker than the other. "I was so afraid for you. But if I'd reached out, the mystic would have known and used you to get to me."

"You trusted me to come here."

"Aye, I know how strong you are."

They kissed then, and it was better than their dreams.

AUTHOR NOTES LUCINDA PEBRE

Thank you for reading my story. I really hope you enjoyed it because I want to write many more. You can find out more about me and what I write at lucindapebre.com

I have no idea how to write *Author Notes*. Yes, I've read enough of Michael's to know what's expected, but somehow that doesn't make it any easier. I understand that this is my chance to talk to the good people who have read my story, but I doubt what I have to say is interesting enough. Still, here goes.

I'm someone who loves to write. Well, of course, I do, else I wouldn't have spent time creating this story. But it's more than that. Sometimes I cannot work out what's in my head without a keyboard under my fingertips, and when it's really bad, a pen in hand. So, to be given the opportunity to write in the KGU, where I've been immersed for a lot of my spare time, makes it really difficult to be able to adequately express my gratitude.

Not only have Michael and the team made it possible,

but they have also supported the process and been incredibly encouraging to us fans attempting this journey. Then, as if that weren't enough, there's the chance for our little stories to be published. Perhaps you can see why it's so difficult to say, "You're awesome."

This was my first attempt at a short story, and it wasn't easy. I struggled with the word limit and found that I had to do the unthinkable and plot. But like anything that takes you out of your comfort zone, I learnt so much.

I wrote the end before going back to the beginning. It reminded me that as a child I always read the end of a book first to make sure the ending was worth slogging through the rest. Sad endings and cliffhangers were always discarded, and that hasn't changed. Fortunately, listening to audiobooks has gotten me out of this bad habit.

When Adaire came to live in my head, she was fully formed. She'd had it rough and could have been a tragic character, but instead of sinking into depression when she lost Calum, she focused on beating the odds in true KGU style.

It took me some time to decide where to set the story. In the end, I chose Justin Sloan's *Hidden Magic Chronicles* because I love Justin's writing and four books were not enough. The series ended far too soon, making it the perfect setting for this story.

Once again, thank you Michael and Justin and all the others who have somehow managed to create a warm and supportive community. I'm so glad to have been a part of it. Long may it continue, now onto the next story.

Lucinda

HAIKU FROM THE KURTHERIAN UNIVERSE

Pod-docs and implants,
Etheric energy too.
We want it all now!

———

Vampires and werewolves
are not natural allies.
BA says, "Who cares?"

BLOOD OF PATRIOTS AND TYRANTS

BY LOGAN CAIRD

This story is different than my others because the mayor in the story, Doctor Fernand Genillon, was the actual mayor of Fismes when the Germans invaded in 1940. He was among those who worked tirelessly against the invaders and helped people escape before he and thirteen others were arrested by the Germans and shipped to concentration camps.

In his case, Buchenwald concentration camp on Ettersberg Hill near Weimar, Germany, over seven hundred kilometers from his home. Those fourteen people, as well as all the others involved in resisting the Nazi occupation, were real French heroes and deserve our praise. I did my best to honor them while using the name of their city, and their mayor, to tell my tale of resistance against oppression. *Vive la liberté*!

BLOOD OF PATRIOTS AND TYRANTS

Fismes, France, June 5, 1940

Fabien Léonide Bouchard heard the rhythmic clinking of a pickaxe on brick from within his coffin. Each *thunk* drew them closer to finding him. Fabien stirred and pushed at the lid of his resting place.

He licked his cracked lips with an equally dry tongue and pushed again and again, timing his efforts against the lid to match the impacts of pick on brick as best as he could.

With one final shove, the seam broke, and the top slid away. He sat up in the small chamber. Whoever was working on the other side of the brick wall had gotten far enough that lines of light gave Fabien a clear view of the room. Dust covered every surface.

The mortaring tools and extra bricks in the corner could barely be seen beneath the layer of dust and mud. Water must have leaked into the room at some point because everything had mud on it.

His arms and legs only slowly responding, he climbed out of the coffin and stretched before looking himself over. His clothing was spotless, far too clean for the chamber he had hidden in. Only his shoes showed any signs of having been in the mud that covered everything else.

He glanced at the thickest part of the mud and started toward it but stopped and shook his head.

The pickaxe broke through a brick. Small pieces of it bounced across the room, one hitting Fabien's shoe. He flicked it away and called, "Careful. That almost hit me."

Fabien could hear someone run out of the room and up the stairs. He shrugged and returned to his coffin, breaking one side off to turn it into a makeshift couch. He sat down on it to wait, wiping some of the mud off his shoes in the interim.

Only a few minutes later he heard someone slowly descend the stairs. A light shone through the hole in the wall and moved across the room. When it reached Fabien, he lifted one hand and waved.

The light jerked back, then returned and settled on his face. He squinted from the brightness but held himself still.

A shocked voice said, "*Fabien?*"

Fabien stood and gave a deep bow. "You have me at a disadvantage, sir."

"I thought you were dead."

Carefully sitting back down and resting his hands where they could be easily seen Fabien said, "I've been in hiding. Took some time away from the world to try to deal with things after the Great War. I don't mean to be rude, but your name?"

"Uh...yes, I am Doctor Fernand Genillon."

Fabien said, "Ferd? You became a doctor? But you hate blood!"

"Yes, and the mayor. Fabien, it has been twenty years since I saw you, but I swear you look exactly the same. I don't have time to be polite. What are you?"

Fabien stood, and the light followed him. He ran a hand through his shoulder-length hair. "That's rather complicated."

Voices from up the stairs called for the doctor. Doctor Genillon snapped off the light and said, "Remain silent. I'll return when I can."

He nearly ran up the stairs, and quietly and carefully closed the door.

The still-bricked-up chamber around Fabien dropped back into darkness. In the building above a handful of people ran around quickly and then all went still.

There was a banging on the door. Loud. Insistent. The muffled voice of the doctor called out that he was coming and one set of footsteps moved across the building.

Fabien returned to his coffin/couch.

Above, a voice snarled something in German. Fabien jerked back to his feet and shot across the room to the opening in the brick wall.

The voice said in thickly German-accented French, "I said, I do not care about your French patients. One of my men has broken his foot, and you will treat him. Now."

"Of course, sir. I'm sorry I do not speak your language. Please, right this way," said the doctor.

Someone stumbled and slid their way across the room above Fabien's head and then dropped heavily onto a couch or bed. The rest of the sounds were so muffled that even with his enhanced hearing, Fabien could make out little. A sudden grunt, then an exclamation of pain.

Sometime later the doctor said, "Keep him off that foot for at least a week, preferably longer. May I return to my other patients now?"

The Germans did not respond, but Fabien heard them cross the room and slam the door on their way out of the building. Those upstairs waited an interminable length of time before moving, only doing so after someone whistled in mimicry of an owl.

The doctor came down the stairs, stopping at the base when he saw Fabien's face pressed against the brick wall. Fabien asked, "What happened? We defeated them."

"It didn't last," the doctor replied. "Listen, Fabien, I do not care what you are. You could be a demon, an angel, or any manner of creature. At this point, all I know is what I remember of you when I was a child. You cannot be worse than what waits above, so I am going to tell everyone that you went into hiding when the Germans took Fismes over a few weeks ago and apologize for not telling them you were in here."

Fabien nodded along with the doctor. "I assure you, I mean no harm."

"As I said, I do not care," the doctor said as he took up the pickaxe and swung at the wall, knocking loose another brick.

Fismes, France, The Home of Doctor Genillon

Fabien climbed through the hole in the wall and followed the doctor upstairs and into his parlor. Some of the furniture looked familiar, but it was all slightly out of place. "You've certainly made my home your own."

"Well, when you go missing for decades, you no longer get to decide who lives in your house."

Fabien shrugged and opened a cabinet, took out a shoe-shining kit, and sat on a couch. He started cleaning off the mud and said, "I meant nothing by it."

"Sorry, it has been a long month. The Germans took Fismes in days. They're using armored vehicles and machine guns this time. We barely put up a fight, and the majority of them have moved on toward Paris."

Pulling out the polish, he applied it to his shoes, "How many did they leave here?"

"Around a hundred men and two of their Panzer tanks. Those are the most dangerous part."

Fabien said, "I should go look these Germans over."

"Walk carefully, Fabien. These German soldiers are not playing around. They will kill you if they catch you spying on them."

"Then they had best not notice me," Fabien replied with a grin.

The doctor, frowning, shook his head. "If you insist on this, you should know that they have taken the Hotel de Ville as their base. One of their Panzers broke down when they were taking over, and they dragged it to the middle of the square near there to use as a guard post. Please be careful, Fabien. There's a curfew so they will shoot you if they see you."

With a last flourish of the polish rag, Fabien said, "Don't worry about me, Ferd. The German's won't expect someone like me."

He left the doctor's house by the back door and moved from shadow to shadow toward the Hotel de Ville. Each time he moved from one building to another he paused to listen. The town was quieter than it should be. Even the Fismois in the homes Fabien passed made as little noise as they could while they moved about.

Nearing the Hotel de Ville, he climbed the side of a mercantile building. Jumping from one rooftop to another, he crossed the remaining dozen buildings. He was on the last building before the square when he saw a figure and froze.

The German, as was obvious from his uniform, was looking down across the square from his perch on the rooftop of a building in the square and had not noticed him. The soldier pointed his gun down as he scanned the road leading to the square.

Fabien jumped onto the same roof as him, landed in a crouch and went still.

The soldier shifted position to get a better view down the road but did not turn around.

Fabien crossed the roof of the building, keeping an eye on the soldier as he stayed on the far side. He didn't look away until he had ducked out of sight behind a chimney.

From here he could see the road leading to the square was torn up. Resting there, fully commanding everything around it, was one of the Panzers. Grey and imposing, the broken tank made a statement. A German soldier sat atop of the tank looking from side to side, his rifle resting across his lap. Another stood on the balcony of the Hotel de Ville across the square.

Two groups of ten soldiers marched into the square

from the far side. They crossed near the tank, and the soldier on the tank saluted, and then they headed into the Hotel de Ville. Fabien watched the building and could see lights turning on and off within it. He couldn't make out anything more than the faint sounds of their voices.

A handful of minutes later, two other groups of soldiers came out of the building and left the square on the near side. They looked well rested and prepared, and headed straight for the building Fabien was on.

He squeezed as close to the chimney as he could.

The soldiers stopped at the base of the building, and the soldier on guard across the roof from him rolled a rope ladder off the building. Someone climbed up it and took the place of the original soldier, who then climbed down and jogged across to the Hotel de Ville. The new soldier pulled the rope ladder back up, and the patrol left the square.

After waiting a few minutes for them to get farther away, Fabien pulled away from the chimney and glanced down at himself. He brushed some soot off his sleeve, blowing at it to try to get the last bit off.

The soldier spun and pointed his rifle at the chimney.

Fabien, still out of sight, heard the sudden movement and dove off the roof. He dropped three floors and hit the ground hard. His left leg snapped with a *crack*, and he rolled out of the alley and around the corner, where he leaned against the wall under an overhang.

The soldier rushed across the roof and looked into the alley, calling out in German. He scanned the area and started toward the side of the building where Fabien was hiding, yelling behind him toward the square.

Fabien popped his leg straight and held it there, and in a few seconds, the bones knit back together. The flesh would take more time but, it would be enough. Favoring that leg, he crossed the road, moving between two buildings into a residential district.

Behind him, German voices called out. They were searching the alley and had found his blood.

Cursing himself, he sped up and ran through the back alleys toward the doctor's house.

Fismes, France

By the time Fabien got to the doctor's house he was fully healed, but his pants were stuck to his leg. He climbed the outside of the house and went into the master bedroom, where he cleaned the wound and got a new pair of pants.

When he stepped out of the closet, the doctor was waiting for him. "Please, take my pants. I'm sure you need them."

Fabien replied, "Mine were damaged."

"They're covered in blood, but you look fine. Did you kill a German?"

"No, it is my blood. I heal quickly."

The doctor held up the pants. The legs were drenched in slowly drying blood. He looked Fabien over and said, "You're pale."

Staying in the closet doorway, as far as he could be from the doctor, Fabien said, "I need something to eat. Healing that injury took a lot."

Eying Fabien, the doctor nodded once and said, "What do you need?"

"Human blood."

"Ah." The doctor said, "Does it need to be, uh...fresh?"

"That would be best, yes."

"Will the donor survive?"

Fabien nodded slightly. "I can limit myself."

The doctor crossed the room and held out his wrist. "Then take what you need."

Moving as slowly as he could, Fabien took the doctor's wrist in his mouth and drank as little as he thought he could get away with. When he was done, the doctor backed away, holding his wrist. "That is all you need? I expected you to take more."

"It will do, thank you, Doctor," Fabien said, bowing deeply. "You need your blood as much as I."

Dropping lightly into a chair, he said, "So, Ferd, I—"

The doctor interrupted him, "Fernand if you must, or doctor, or even mayor. No one has called me Ferd in quite some time."

"Sorry, doctor. I was able to get a look at the disposition of the Germans. Would I be correct in saying that you have people hiding in this house?"

"Yes. That was why we were digging in the cellar. We realized that the brick wall was not external, and hoped to find a place to hide more people. There are thirty here who need to remain out of German hands at all costs. The Germans are not well disposed toward the Jews or the Roma."

Crossing one foot over a knee, Fabien wiped at his shoe and said, "As I thought, though I didn't know the specifics. I saw a hole in the Germans' patrol. There's a half-hour period when their patrols are all in the Hotel de Ville as they change over. If we move during that time, we should be able to get them out of town without being noticed."

"How certain of this are you?"

"Completely. The guards waiting outside the Hotel de Ville were expecting it. That tells me it must happen at the same time each night—a couple of hours after midnight."

The doctor started absently as he washed the blood out of the pants and said, "If we take them north, moving away from the town square, it will give us extra time. Once in the countryside, they can spread out and go to ground. It's the best we can do."

"While everyone is moving, I can keep an eye out for any Germans. With my capabilities, I can move across the rooftops, and should be able to hear them coming long before they can see us."

The doctor spread the pants on a rod to dry and said, "Very well, but now I need to sleep. There's a bed in the spare room you can use."

"Thank you, but I will need to sleep on the..." Fabien paused, "on the couch in the cellar. I cannot chance exposure to the sun."

"As long as you don't mind sharing. The people I mentioned are down there now."

Fabien shrugged. "I'll make do."

Fismes, France, Cellar of Genillon Home

Bang!

Fabien jerked awake at the sound from above.

The front door to the house slammed open and German voices called, "Doctor! Get down here."

In his groggy state and surrounded by the huddled

mass of people, he couldn't tell how many came in, but it was quite a few. They stomped around the building, pulling open cabinets and looking through closets. In the room with him, a mother started bouncing a baby on her knee to keep it quiet.

From above, the doctor said in a muffled voice, "Sorry, I was asleep. What's wrong?"

"Show me the injured. Someone was spying on us last night. They were badly injured escaping, and I will find them," the German commander snarled.

"Of course, sir. They are all right back this way. They are the same ones who were here yesterday. No one new."

"I'll be the judge of that," the commander snapped.

Fabien pulled back against the side of his coffin, knowing exactly who they were looking for.

The soldiers continued searching the house as the doctor took the commander to the back and showed him the injured people. The doctor said, "All these are sick with diseases. I wouldn't touch them."

A voice called out in pain, and the commander said, "Aha! Show me your leg!"

There was coughing, over which the doctor said, "Let me."

Fabien heard a gasp and gagging noise, then the doctor said, "As I said, disease. His leg is rotting, not broken."

From where he lay, as still as he could be, Fabien heard the commander stumble out of the house and retch in the backyard. He pushed himself in order to try to remain awake, but in the middle of the day, it was hard. He faded in and out of awareness as the soldiers searched the rest of the house.

They didn't find the hidden staircase that led to the cellar, and by the time they left Fabien was deeply asleep.

Fismes, France

After the sun set, the doctor came down into the cellar. Fabien was sitting in his coffin, a Roma child in his arms as he swayed back and forth. She leaned against his chest and sucked on her thumb. The child's mother, who was feeding her son a few feet away, glanced up as the doctor came into the room.

The doctor said, "Time to get ready. The patrol should be heading back to the Hotel de Ville in the next half-hour. At that point, we can leave."

Heads nodded around the room. A Roma man stood up and said, "We have been talking," motioning with his head to a group of four young men near him, "and we are not going with you. We want to stay in Fismes to fight the Germans."

The doctor said, "Are you sure? This may be the last chance to leave for a long time."

"We are sure."

"That may help us tonight. Can the five of you stay in nearby buildings and watch for the patrol? If they come earlier than we expect, try to draw them off. It will be dangerous, but it could help the rest of the people here get out of town safely."

The young man stood straighter, glanced at his friends, and nodded. "Yes, we can do that. We will not let them find you!"

Fabien said, "Don't risk too much. Just draw them away and then hide. Don't get yourself killed."

His face set, the young man assured him, "We will not let them find you." His friends stood up, and one put a hand on his shoulder before nodding. The five of them left the house to find places to watch from.

Fabien handed the child in his arms back to her mother. "I'll go make sure that the patrol is changing shift. I'll meet you back here shortly."

The doctor waved him off and started helping people pack.

Fabien headed toward the town square, being more careful than the night before. He didn't need to get all the way there to be sure of their schedule. As long as the patrol was heading in that direction, it should be fine.

He climbed onto the roof of the first tall building he came to and looked for the patrols. He couldn't see them, but a short time later he heard them several streets over.

Taking a running start, he cleared the street and rolled to a stop on a roof closer to the patrol. After standing and brushing himself off, he found that he had a good vantage and looked down the street. A squad of German soldiers, ten in total, was a hundred meters away.

As they passed each building, they checked any dark spots, looked down alleys, and gazed into the ground-floor windows. A member of the squad with a machine gun had remained in the middle of the street at all times, shoulders tight, looking ahead. The final soldier in line walked backward with a rifle at the ready and several grenades on his belt. Every few seconds one of the soldiers would lift his rifle and scan the windows and rooftops.

Fabien backed away from the edge of the building as the patrol passed. He stayed out of sight, hearing them go farther toward the square. When he could no longer hear them, he climbed down off the building and returned to the doctor's house.

Rounding the corner to approach the house from behind, Fabien couldn't see anyone, but he could hear the breathing of dozens of people. He walked into the yard with his hands out and softly said, "It's me."

The doctor stood from behind a rose bush and asked, "Well?"

"The patrols are returning to the Hotel de Ville. We can go, but should hurry."

Everyone rose from wherever they were hiding in bushes, doorways, and even from below the stairs. The doctor led the way, and Fabien took up the rear. Things went smoothly as they passed through the yards behind houses, over several streets, and toward the north part of town.

Across the street, the first of the young men waved at Fabien and ducked into an alley. He was holding a long metal rod that looked like a fence pole. Fabien waved back, then jogged to catch up to the rest of the group.

At each road they crossed, the doctor would hold everyone up for a few moments to check both ways and listen, making sure no soldiers lurked out of sight. Every few blocks he saw another of the young men, each with their own improvised weapon.

When the buildings started to thin out, Fabien both heard and saw the last of the five young men who were staying behind peel off to head back toward the main part of town. It looked like he carried a sword. The doctor led the group into the next street and across, heading toward the La Vesle river a few blocks away.

Snap, crack!

A piece of the road near Fabien shot into the air as the sound of a gunshot reached him. A hundred meters away, just at the end of the road, a squad of German soldiers was running toward them. Their rifles in hand, they moved a short distance and stopped to fire before hurrying toward the fleeing group again.

Fabien yelled, "Run!"

All pretense of stealth was lost. The fugitives sprinted outright toward the river. Fabien saw the mother of two struggling with her children. Putting on a burst of speed, he scooped up the young boy, all of five years old, and ran with him to the doctor. He said, "Here! Carry him, and I will try to lead them away."

Child in hand, the doctor led the rest toward the river. Fabien returned to the corner of the building. On the way, he picked up a few loose cobbles from the road.

Fismes, France, Near the La Vesle River

Staying out of sight Fabien waited at the corner of the building. The soldiers were running full out and would be there in a moment. Too soon for those fleeing to escape. Closing his eyes, he waited. When it sounded like they were only a short distance away, he spun around the corner and threw the cobblestones at the soldiers as hard as he could.

The soldiers dove out of the way. Most of the stones missed, but one slammed into the helmeted head of a soldier several back in line. It hit with enough force to flip the soldier end over end. Fabien sprinted back toward town before that soldier hit the ground, dead.

Gunshots sounded behind him, and bullets zipped past him, but none struck home before he made it out of sight. He ran to the end of the alley, scooping up more cobblestones as he went, and waited.

Even though he was much faster than them, the soldiers only took a few seconds to reach the alley.

Fabien was preparing to throw the cobblestones again when the machine gunner stepped into view, firing as he moved into the alley. The gun kicked and bucked in his hands, making it impossible for him to aim, but it was enough.

Fabien dropped the cobblestones and dove out of the way. One round from the machine gun clipped the back of his leg and sent him sprawling. He scrambled to his feet and stumbled across the street, the back of his leg quickly closing up.

The machine gun stopped firing after a few seconds, and the soldiers chased him. They made it to the street as he made it to the alley and charged toward him, bayonets leading the way. The machine gunner ran up last.

Most of the soldiers didn't fire as they were running, not being accurate enough, and Fabien used that to full advantage. He ducked behind every obstacle he could find. He knocked down barrels and jumped over fences. As he cleared one fence, the squad leader fired two shots from his pistol, one of which hit him in the shoulder and sent him sprawling again.

At that point, he started to worry he wouldn't have enough blood in him to be able to make it back to the fleeing people. He picked up speed, dove over the next few fences, and ran into an alley.

As he ducked from view, the soldiers opened fire again. Bullets slammed into the walls around him. Over the sound of bullets, he heard a *clink, thud, thud* sound as a grenade rolled to a stop a few feet away.

He threw himself up the side of the building and reached the top in a single jump, then sprinted across it and leapt toward the next building. When he was mid-air, he heard it go off. The grenade blew apart the fence and a corner of the building. He landed in a roll and ran for the next roof, and the next, aiming for buildings that would give him quick passage but leave the Germans far behind. Soon he couldn't even hear them running, so he circled around to try to catch up with the rest of the fleeing people.

Fismes, France, Near the La Vesle River

Hopping from one roof to another, Fabien tracked back along his path. He only climbed down to the ground when the buildings got too far apart. He didn't see any of the fleeing people, but also didn't see any bodies or smell any blood, so he took it as a good sign.

He made it to the bridge across the river before he heard any people moving—running boots from more soldiers on the other side of the river. He sprinted across the bridge and ran toward the sounds of shouting German voices.

Rounding a corner, he saw them—another squad of German soldiers. They had the escapees backed against a building. All twenty-six of them, including the doctor. The soldier's rifles were raised.

Fabien screamed and charged. He slammed into the back of the first soldier he came to, shoulder first. The man's back *snapped*, and he dropped to the ground. Fabien scooped up his rifle, and all the soldiers turned on him.

The squad leader fired his pistol directly into Fabien's chest, making him stumble back a few steps. Four soldiers charged him, leading with bayonets. Fabien righted himself and swung his captured rifle wildly.

The lead soldier couldn't react quickly enough, and the rifle slammed into his head and broke his neck, but the following soldier jumped forward and stabbed Fabien in the arm. From the other side, another soldier stabbed him in the side of his chest.

He rolled backward still holding half a rifle. The soldiers followed, more of them catching up. His wounds started healing and he threw the rifle butt at the next soldier in line, knocking him to the ground, then grabbed the rifle of another soldier. The soldier wouldn't let go, so he swung the rifle, soldier and all, to the side.

The soldier let go of his rifle as a bayonet slammed into his back from his charging companion.

Crack!

Another round slammed into Fabien. The squad leader was calmly walking around the melee shooting him whenever there was a clear shot. Fabien snarled and threw the rifle he was holding at the squad leader.

He telegraphed his throw too clearly, though, and the squad leader took a single step back. The rifle shot past him and shattered against the wall almost fifty feet away, so he shot Fabien again.

Another soldier dove forward and stabbed Fabien, who kicked him in the chest and yanked the rifle from his hand. He flew across the street and slammed into the wall, slumping to the ground, unmoving.

Crack!

Yet another round slammed into his shoulder, sending Fabien spinning to the ground. Two of the remaining soldiers stabbed down at him with their bayonets, and he tried to roll out of the way, but only dodged one. The other went through his leg, pinning him in place.

With a twist he snapped the blade off the bayonet, leaving it in his leg as he rolled forward and tackled the soldier. He hefted him off the ground and bit his neck, and blood shot into his mouth. He backed up, holding the soldier he was draining between him and the rest of the squad.

The squad leader shot the soldier in Fabien's hands in the back of the head, ending his life. The blood rushed through Fabien's body, closing his many wounds, but he was slower now. *Only four left,* he thought, eying them.

He ran toward the squad leader, holding the corpse like a shield. Seconds before reaching the leader, he threw the body toward the next nearest soldier.

The squad leader got one last shot off before Fabien grabbed his head and spun him around, throwing him at another soldier. The shot went wide but distracted the soldier who was chasing him.

Scooping up the pistol, Fabien turned to the next

soldier and pulled the trigger. *Click*. Empty. "Are you kidding me?"

The three remaining soldiers opened fire. Two shots slammed into him and knocked him down. The third went wide, striking the building against which all the escapees were cowering.

Fabien ran forward and tackled two of the soldiers. He punched them as quickly as he could, alternating between them to keep them from fighting back. One went still, and he turned to the other but felt a sharp pain as the last soldier slammed his bayonet into Fabien's back.

He rolled forward off the blade, his wound starting to close, then ran straight back. He tackled the soldier who had stabbed him and crushed his windpipe.

Standing over the squad of dead soldiers, Fabien panted. The night became strangely quiet. Even the Fismois were still.

The silence was broken by the growl of a petrol engine from the direction of the bridge.

Fabien turned toward the river, mouth hanging open, as the Panzer drove toward them. He yelled, "RUN!" and charged toward the tank.

The Panzer driving toward him had two machine guns and a cannon on the front. As it crossed the bridge, the machine guns spun up, and rounds chewed across the ground toward Fabien. Cobblestones shattered and shards flew into the air in a cloud.

He dove to the side, came up in a roll, and sprinted toward the building, away from the fleeing Fismois. The machine gun followed him, blowing holes in the building.

He pushed himself to vampiric speed as he ran toward the tank.

He jumped high into the air and slammed onto the tank. It continued after the fleeing civilians.

He started punching the top, each slam of his fist causing fractures to his bones as well as penetrating the metal of the tank.

The sky acquired a sudden red hue. Dawn was coming.

Fabien clambered across the top of the tank and grabbed the barrels of the two machine guns. They were still firing, turning to follow the doctor. He bent the barrels of both of them back on themselves mid-shot. They exploded, knocking him off the tank and causing the driver to skid to the side.

Hands bleeding, Fabien hopped to his feet and sprinted toward the tank. On the way, he ripped a metal fence post out of the ground, then jumped as high as he could and slammed the post into the fuel tank of the Panzer.

Petrol shot out and covered Fabien as well as most of the vehicle, but it righted itself and continued after the people running away. They had crossed to another street, and the tank was circling back toward them.

Fabien looked at the doctor and the fuel tank, and then up at the rising sun. He screamed and grabbed the hole in the tank and started to pull. Metal peeled back, making the opening larger.

The sun rose above the roof of the farthest building, and as its light touched his skin, it started to burn. The outer layers turning to ash, Fabien's body burned. The fumes from the petrol rising from the tank touched him and ignited. The entire tank went up in flames as it shot down the road, out of control, and sank into the river as the doctor and twenty-five people escaped into the countryside.

That was the last time the doctor saw Fabien Léonide Bouchard.

Thank you for reading one of the first, though hopefully not the last, of my writings in the Kurtherian Gambit Universe. For a number of reasons, this short story hit home. I've been to war. I was in the Marines for five years, deployed to Iraq twice for a combined total of eighteen months. During that time, I was shot at, nearly blown up, and saw people shot. It was chance alone that I didn't see anyone die. When I sat down to write this, I felt a need to treat it with respect, and I hope I did it justice.

I hope you liked my story. I look forward to having more to tell. If you liked it enough to want to hear from me, please stop by my site LoganCaird.com and sign up for my mailing list, or follow me on Facebook at Logan Caird. I'll let you know, through both of those, when I write anything new.

HAIKU FROM THE KURTHERIAN UNIVERSE

Choose Coke or Pepsi?
You must select rightly, or
You shall be punished!

ANYONE FOR JUICE

BY DOMINIC NOVIELLI

Armi' is only seven but has enough gumption to be much older. With Conrey, her best and only friend, who she wants to cheer up, after his mother was killed a short time back, by getting his very own anti-gravity sled with translucent holo controls. The only thing stopping her is having enough credits. She happens upon a lucrative business selling juice but there is a problem, it's addictive and all the Noel-Ni's on the space station want some every day.

Take a read and see how Armi' handles big business and if she's successful at getting Conrey his sled. And of course her ever present Geddon, as long as she remembers to bring her along, is constantly at her side or she me find her jumpsuits glued together at the legs and arms.

CHAPTER ONE

WHAT TO DO ABOUT CONREY?

"Mom?"

"Yes, dear, what is it?" Armi's mother looked down at her with sympathetic eyes.

"What can I do for Conrey?" Armi huffed and smacked the small dining table with both fists, then laid her head down between them. She was trying to figure out a way to help her best friend.

Her mother walked up behind Armi and bent down to hug her little girl.

"I'm not sure, dear. What do *you* think? Any ideas in that turbulent head of yours?"

"Oh, I don't know. Arghhh!" Armi cried, banging her fists on the tabletop again. Her mother cringed but didn't say anything.

With a raised eyebrow, her mother asked, "Did you ask Geddon, by chance? She has great ideas." Armi's mom's face wore a look of hope, but when Armi nodded, her expression went flat.

"Oh, dear." Her mother sighed.

"I'm going to bed. Maybe I will dream about something I can't think of while I'm awake." With a defeated look, Armi stomped into the only room in the small apartment, her bedroom.

She felt bad about having left Geddon on the bed that morning. "Hey, Geddon. Sorry for leaving you this morning. My mind was on trying to cheer Conrey up, and I've failed miserably at that." Armi trudged to the small bed and collapsed next to Geddon. Her father had picked up the Empress Bethany Anne doll on his travels and installed an EI within it. After she and Conrey had a bit of trouble and having Conrey's mother pass away, she had finally named her doll "Geddon," as in "Armi-Geddon." She liked the play on words.

"What do you think? Any ideas since this morning about how to cheer Conrey up?" She looked expectantly at Geddon.

I do have a few ideas, but the main one is to get Conrey something he wants. That would take his mind off his mother being gone. I believe Conrey wants an antigrav sled with holo controls. Is that correct?

"I think you may be onto something." Armi smiled, thinking of the look on Conrey's face as he gazed at his new antigrav sled and played with the translucent holo controls. Her face fell immediately, though.

"Damn, who am I kidding? Those things cost a lot of credits, and in case you haven't noticed, we don't have any." She grimaced and pushed her head into her pillow to yell out her frustration without disturbing the entire space station.

Armi, I don't believe yelling is going to solve your problem. What have we been going over in school the past few days?

If Geddon *could* issue a reprimand, she would have used a voice like that. Armi, ashamed of having yelled like that, looked at the floor instead of Geddon. "I'm sorry, Geddon, but I am out of ideas. I know the Empress would not give in. She would come up with a kick-ass plan to get Conrey his sled."

So, what do you think we could do to get the sled? There are many ways to get credits. Let me calculate your chances of getting the amount of credit you need by doing the odd jobs on the space station, and how long it would take to accumulate the required amount.

"Calculate all you want. It won't make a difference. That sled is way too much. It would take years to earn enough." With a defeated look, Armi thought about her father and what he was doing at that moment. It had been months since he had been home, and she missed him.

"Geddon?" Armi asked the EI.

Yes, Armi? How can I be of service?

Armi picked the doll up and cradled her in her arms. "You will never leave me, will you?" A look of dread crossed Armi's face, and she had a deep sadness settled into the pit of her stomach, which felt like she ate a black hole.

I will never leave you, Armi. We are friends, are we not? No, we are sisters, since your father created me.

Geddon was silent after that sage comment, and she hugged Geddon to her and closed her eyes. With a slight smile, she fell into a dream of Conrey and her gliding down the station's halls on a new deep-purple antigrav sled with holo controls.

CHAPTER TWO

AN IDEA ABOUT JUICE

Armi woke up early, ate her breakfast of nutrients and lamnas bread, and took a quick sonic shower in the shared bathroom area. After dressing, she took off, leaving her mother swaddled in blankets on the makeshift sofa that her dad had put together for her mother and him as their bed. Armi quietly shut the door and with a gloomy expression went over to see Conrey. She was going to try to get him to take an interest in something. *Anything*.

"Conrey, are you there? Open the god-for-damit door already!" Armi yelled, knocking several times on the door to his father's and his living quarters. Before Armi could yell again, she heard the door lock click and saw the latch twist.

"Conrey, It's Armi. Let me in."

"Why? There's nobody here," Conrey replied in a slug-gish voice with zero enthusiasm. Armi shook her head and pushed the door open. Conrey was thrown back by the strength Armi used and landed on his backside. He glared at her as he got off the floor.

"Well, that's a better look on you. I'd rather you get angry than see that god-awful sorry-ass bistok-poop-eating depressed look that's been on your face lately." Armi smirked at him and plopped down on their *real* couch. Before Conrey's mother had passed, she'd worked for that screwed up big wig Noel-ni, Papyon, and she had made good credit while it lasted. With that job and the engineering Conrey's father did for the space station, they had enough credits to afford the better things in life.

Conrey almost smiled at Armi's flagrant use of swear words. He thought she could impress the Empress with her vulgarity.

"Armi, what do you want? It's not a good time. I'd rather be alone." Conrey repeated the same excuses in the same bland tone he'd been using for the last few months. Armi was sick of it and glared daggers at Conrey with her violet eyes. Armi was part-Torcellan and part-Kezzin, which should not have been possible. She was a beautiful girl of seven with light reddish skin up to her neck, and from there her coloring changed to a light burnt orange color, making her face look as if she had gotten the best tan of her life. She had no hair, like her Kezzin father, but rather a cartilage structure on her head that looked like a hat or a crown, if you saw her from a distance.

"Conrey!" Armi growled. Conrey backed up a little with a worried expression. "I'm only going to say this once. You're coming with me today, or I swear by the Empress' teats that you and I will trade blows until one of us isn't walking anymore." The look Armi gave Conrey left no doubt that she meant every word. Conrey gulped loudly and nodded.

"Okay, then, let's be off." Armi chirped, her anger instantly gone. Conrey let out the breath he didn't know he had been holding in a huge sigh. He meekly followed Armi out the door.

"First stop, Mrs. Gatoroid's fruit stand," Armi told Conrey pleasantly over her shoulder as she skipped toward the central chamber where shopkeepers on the station sold their wares. The lower levels of the rotunda were designed in large concentric circles. They were in the center of the station, so there was no looking at the stars from there even if you wanted to, although most didn't care. They were so far from known civilization that the station didn't even have a proper name. It was just called "the space station," or at least that was all Armi or Conrey had ever heard it called. As Armi skipped ahead, and Conrey shuffled behind, Mrs. Gatoroid finished with a few customers.

Mrs. Gatoroid's fruit stand was one of a kind. She was an older Torcellan who traveled about searching for exotic fruit to stock her stands and on one of her expeditions came across *the station*. Armi didn't know why she even bothered with this station but was glad she did. Every once in a while, when the customer traffic died down, she would tell Armi, Geddon, and Conrey stories of the Empress and her Bitches.

"Hey there, Mrs. Gatoroid. How is the fruit business?" Armi pleasantly asked the distinguished lady, who was wearing a very new jumpsuit, while the last group of customers walked away chatting.

"Why, if it isn't my favorite youngsters! Visiting an old

lady to make her final days sunnier?" She laughed, and the sparkle in her eyes made Armi smile. Conrey was still gloomy. He stood looking down at his feet, apparently finding them very interesting at that moment.

With a knowing look, Mrs. Gatoroid picked up a large berry type fruit and tossed it to Conrey. "Catch, young man. If it hits the ground, you get to clean it up." Conrey quickly looked up and barely grabbed the firm fruit before it was too late.

"Good catch, Conrey." Armi smiled at him, which he didn't return. He grimaced instead. "You're impossible." Armi threw her hands up in exasperation and blew out a noisy breath. Mrs. Gatoroid chuckled and handed one of the fruits to Armi.

"Here ya go, young lady. A growing girl needs her vitamins. Those berries carry a large dose of what ya need." She winked at Armi and sat on a chair next to her stand.

"What shall it be today, an Empress saga, or one about a fight for Justice with the Bitches giving a beating to those who deserved it?" She looked at Conrey, who shrugged as he ate. The pink juice dripped down his chin, which he didn't seem to notice, but he did seem to enjoy the sweet fruit. Armi was a little more cautious and kept her mouth clean by only taking small bites.

"The Bitches for sure!" Armi replied enthusiastically and giggled. With a fond smile, Mrs. Gatoroid began her tale just as another group of customers walked over.

"Ah, Mrs. Gatoroid, a pleasure as always." A slender businessman with short hair and a clean-shaven face smiled at Armi as he greeted Mrs. Gatoroid. Those with him stood silently while he conducted his business. "Do you have the containers we discussed last quarter?"

"I do, I do. Let me see, where did I put them?" Mrs. Gatoroid tapped her chin for a moment then started pulling up tarps that covered a multitude of boxes. "Ah, here we go." She waved the man over to show him his prize with a celebratory smile.

"I believe we negotiated a slightly higher price for removing the contents before delivery, not ones still containing fruit." The man went from pleasant to all business in the blink of an eye.

"Oh, dear. Was that what we agreed to? Well, if that was the case I'll remove the fruit for ya, but it will take me today and part of tomorrow to finish. I hope that will not be too much of an inconvenience?" Mrs. Gatoroid put her hands together as if praying and looked sheepishly up at the man. He was at least a foot taller than her.

"Fine, fine. I'll send someone around suppertime tomorrow to pick up the crate." He shook her hand and quickly left with his entourage in pursuit as he walked to the gravity lifts at the side of the rotunda.

"Wow, that was a little intense," Armi exclaimed, looking into the crate of fruit the man had ordered.

"Not really. I remembered our deal. I was just hoping he hadn't." Mrs. Gatoroid scratched her head. "Well, my dear, the story will have to wait. I have a lot of work to accomplish. Sorry, but work is work."

"Ah, Mrs. Gatoroid, can Conrey and me help you? That is, we'll help for a little credit," Armi asked, looking sweet and unassuming.

Mrs. Gatoroid looked Armi up and down, did the same to Conrey, and finally nodded in agreement. "A credit per empty fruit container, and there are about a hundred and fifty of them." The fruit seller raised her eyebrows at them, waiting for the youngsters to back out because they had bitten off more than they could chew. Armi was determined to make enough money to get Conrey that antigrav sled, and put her hand out to seal the deal. She looked over at Conrey, who was stubbing his foot into the deck plating and felt a mixture of emotions well up inside.

Mrs. Gatoroid showed them which tools to use. First, they had to make a small hole with one tool, and then they used another that looked like a thin metal gun. When the trigger was depressed, a bunch of whips came out of the end and spun. You put the tip of the gun to the hole, and the whips went through it and mashed up the fruit. When the fruit was properly liquefied, the tool was removed, and the contents could be emptied by turning it over a barrel to catch the thin yellow pulp and juice.

"This is fun, isn't that right, Conrey?" Armi asked him sarcastically.

"It's ok, I guess."

Armi was going to make Conrey happy if it killed her. Armi growled at him and went back to draining the fruit. After a few of them were done, Armi dipped her finger into the juice to taste it.

"Ugh! That tastes terrible!" *Plooey, plaw, plaw.* Armi spat the juice onto the floor.

"Doesn't taste very good, does it, dear?" Mrs. Gatoroid asked Armi as she came from the back of the booth. "Well, it's only been a few minutes, and I see you have already done ten of them. Very good, very good. At that pace, you may be done by tonight." She smiled at Armi and Conrey. "You know, it might make it more palatable if you combined that bland juice with a really sweet one. I've never had a reason to try since the deal was for the container rather than what was in it." She looked again at the finished empty fruit containers and let out a satisfied sigh, giving them a soft smile as she walked over to greet new customers.

The combining of juices gave Armi an idea, and she whispered her idea to Conrey. "How about we mix berry juice, maybe from the one we had earlier, with the juice from this one? If it tastes good, we can sell it and make a load of credit." Armi was excited about the idea, but Conrey's mood was putting a damper on her excitement. She frowned at him and waited for Mrs. Gatoroid to be free so that she could ask for another berry and taste-test her idea.

A short time later, with the mixed juices. "Well?" Armi asked Conrey, after he took a sip.

"It's ok. Not anything special, but it's refreshing, and I feel a little better just tasting it." Conrey was subdued with his emotions, and his response grated on Armi's nerves.

She huffed. "You could be a little more enthusiastic about it."

"It's okay. It's worth a credit to me." Conrey was trying to placate Armi, but he knew she had an agenda and he had nothing to do with it—which made him that much more depressed.

"Ok, then. Mrs. Gatoroid said we can have the pulp insides, and she will still pay us. And, since we need the berry to make the stuff sweeter, she agreed to give us enough berries to make the whole batch palatable." Armi had a tough time pronouncing that last word—palatable. She'd had to say it several times when she'd heard Mrs. Gatoroid use it.

CHAPTER THREE

MAKING MORE THAN A KILLING

After they'd emptied all the fruit containers, it was dinner-time for Conrey and Armi, and they had to get home.

"You did a marvelous job, and I'll have the credits for you tomorrow. If you plan on selling the juice, why not use my stand? I have plenty of room, and you could buy the cups you'll need from the stand a couple of stalls down." Mrs. Gatoroid liked both youngsters and had to commend them on their entrepreneurial spark. Plus, she had always wanted to see how a juice stand would work alongside her fruit. She made a mental note to put the saltier fruits out front tomorrow. She waved to the kids and returned to work, happy now that the work was completed earlier than expected.

When Armi arrived home, she remembered she had forgotten Geddon again in her hurry that morning. She wouldn't be surprised if Geddon was very upset with her. She would be.

"Geddon, you should be mad at me for forgetting you,

yet again?" Armi whispered as she slowly opened the door to her room.

Not really, I've been busy. I have uncovered several jobs that you and Conrey would be able to perform. You could charge a much lower rate than others, but you would still make enough to purchase the antigravity sled you want Conrey to have. By my calculations, it will only take four years and three months.

"I hate to break it to you, but I will be an old lady by then." Armi smiled at Geddon. "Conrey and I have a business already, thanks to Mrs. Gatoroid. You will never guess what we are going to sell tomorrow." She had a smug smile on her face that dared Geddon to answer correctly.

You will be selling fruit juice, I suspect, but that's only a guess on my part.

"How in the heck did you come up with that? You smug bit…." Armi threw her hands up and jumped onto the bed beside Geddon. With her hands behind her head, she stared at Geddon with a quizzical expression.

I take it I was correct?

"Yes, you were. How did you do that?" Armi asked more politely this time.

You have fruit stains on your jumpsuit and I calculated the probability of how you got them, knowing that you would be seeing Mrs. Gatoroid at some point. Therefore, it seemed a good choice to pick fruit juice.

"You are amazing, you know that, Geddon? I love you for your mind, even though you do have Empress Bethany Anne's body."

It's a small artificial version of her body, but I agree. Just remember that my incredible intelligence will not be able to help you if you keep leaving without me.

The next morning Armi was once again up early, but this time she grabbed Geddon before she went to pick up Conrey.

"You ready?" Armi asked her friend when he answered his door.

"I guess," Conrey replied in the same dull, lifeless voice he'd used since his mother had died.

You know she will always be with you. You carry her DNA in you. Geddon told Conrey, using the stations floor speakers, as he followed Armi to the rotunda.

"I know you're right, but it's not the same. If we had only been a couple of minutes earlier, we could have saved her." Conrey's expression was troubled.

"Listen up, you hair-brained bistok reject, enough with this what-if crap. We did all that we could. Nothing short of a miracle would have saved your mother. She died trying to get others to safety. Remember what the investigators said? You should be proud of her. I am."

Armi poked Conrey in the chest as she rattled off each point, then softened her voice and grabbed Conrey by both arms. "You need to let go of your 'what if we had been a little quicker?' If your mother had had more time, what do you think she would have done with it? Run to safety?" Armi shook him, then stepped back to wait for his answer with her arms crossed on her chest, leaning to one side and giving him dagger eyes. It was Armi's signature look.

This time, Conrey thought about what his mother would have done if she'd had more time, and what he came up with put a smile on his face.

"She would have saved even more people," he replied with more jubilance and energy in his voice. Armi smirked and let out a snort, then did an abrupt about-face, and they continued their trek to Mrs. Gatoroid's stand.

As they prepared the juice, they wondered how the heck a pink fruit and a yellow fruit could produce a purple drink when mixed. Mrs. Gatoroid started spouting off chemical combinations that would make that happen until Armi tuned her out and focused on mixing the combination of pulp and sweet berry juice making a heavy syrup like liquid.

Mrs. Gatoroid recommended diluting the thickened contents with water, which had an added benefit of increasing the amount of juice they could sell.

Both Armi and Conrey had been pleasantly surprised to find a table set up for them and a few rows of empty cups stacked to the side. They put the purple juice on the table in a metal dispenser Mrs. Gatoroid provided them that had a glass center so that they could see when it was getting low.

"Mrs. Gatoroid, you shouldn't have. Thank you very much for doing this, but it's too much." Armi narrowed her eyes. "How much for all this? Did the money we made yesterday cover it?" Armi held her breath as she waited for Mrs. Gatoroid's answer.

"Oh, my dear, the cups were only a couple of credits, and the table I'd left here ages ago and completely forgot about it until last night. Don't worry; you still have plenty of credits coming your way." Mrs. Gatoroid walked by her and patted her on the shoulder with a motherly grin and slight squeeze as she continued forward to greet new customers.

"How much for the juice?" a Noel-ni of middle years

asked Conrey, who was behind the table getting the cups set up.

"A credit a cup," Conrey told him. Armi noticed a credit recorder behind the row of cups; Mrs. Gatoroid thought of everything.

"You think that's for us, Geddon?" Armi asked her doll.

Yes. There is no other reason for it being there other than to receive payment for your purple passion juice.

"'Purple Passion Juice.' That's hilarious—I like it. Hey, Conrey! How about we call the stuff Purple Passion Juice?" Armi laughed as she threw the credit reader to him.

"Sounds good," he answered in the usual monotone voice, catching the reader and finishing the sale. She was going to kick his ass if he didn't cheer up. Armi growled but quickly plastered on a smile as more customers came over to buy their purple juice.

By the end of the day, repeat buyers were coming back to purchase more. Both Armi and Conrey were ecstatic. Conrey was even smiling. "Mrs. Gatoroid, can you tell us the number of sales we made today?" Armi asked her with a greedy look that was more playful than real.

Mrs. Gatoroid smiled at them and punched a few buttons on her wrist holo. With a huge grin, she told them, "Final count is two hundred and twenty credits. Congratulations! That is an impressive first day. It usually takes more time to build a clientele that large." Mrs. Gatoroid nodded and kept smiling at them as she read off the numbers.

At this rate, you will make the amount you need in...

Armi cut off Geddon's reply. "Don't say anything to Conrey. It's a secret, so no blabbing," she whispered to

Geddon, leaning toward her doll's ear so that Conrey would not hear. Conrey was currently taking the table they'd used to the back as Mrs. Gatoroid closed up shop. Being a Noel-ni, he had exceptional hearing.

Sorry, my mistake, Geddon whispered back, using the speaker imbedded inside the doll.

Mrs. Gatoroid winked at Armi. "I'll keep the secret. No worries, dear."

CHAPTER FOUR

UNEXPECTED RESULTS

After dropping Conrey off, Armi skipped the rest of the way home.

"Mom, guess what?" Armi started shouting even before the door was open. Her mother was at the makeshift stove as she always was. She'd told Armi that since the station was always cold to her, this was the only way she felt warm.

"What, my little miracle?" her mother asked as she turned toward Armi.

"Guess what Conrey and I did today? You will never believe it! We made two hundred and twenty credits selling juice," Armi told her mother with a huge grin.

"You what?" Delani exclaimed with a total look of disbelief. "How?"

Delani just stared at Armi with her mouth open. After a few minutes, Armi got a little worried. "Are you ok, Mom?" Armi asked with concern in her voice.

"Mom, we worked with Mrs. Gatoroid, and she helped

set it all up. You see, she had these fruit things that needed to be drained, and Conrey and I asked if we could do it, and then everything just fell into place." Armi hoped her mother would snap out of whatever trance she was in and at least talk to her now that she had explained.

"Armi, you made two hundred credits in one *day*?" Delani put a hand to her face, "Oh, my, that is incredible. How old are you again?" her mom asked her with a nervous laugh.

"You know how old I am; I'm seven. Don't be silly." Armi grimaced and shook her head.

"I'm being silly? A seven-year-old girl makes more money than all the men on this space station, and you tell me that *I'm* being silly?"

"What's wrong with that? I want to help Conrey, and this is a way to do that. It's all legal and everything. At least, I think it's legal. Mrs. Gatoroid wouldn't steer us wrong." Armi had a little doubt in her voice. Geddon had taught Armi about ethics a few months ago after the bombs went off outside the rotunda. Geddon had wanted to strike while the iron was hot. It made sense to Armi how people should care about what their business practices did to others. Armi was thinking of that when her mother motioned for her to come close.

"Come here, Armi. I want to hold you and stop you from growing up."

"That's absurd, Mom. How can you stop me from growing up?" Armi had a puzzled expression on her face, but her mother just smiled and pulled her into a smothering hug.

There is a way to make it so that Armi will grow very slowly.

A Pod-doc could make the nanocytes slow your aging process and extend your life by a number of years.

"Thank you very much, Geddon, but I don't think that will be necessary. I want to grow up and be as beautiful as my mother." Armi scolded Geddon. The look on Delani's face after Armi's confession was priceless. She had tears in her eyes as she rocked them both back and forth.

"Oh, my little girl is all grown up. I love you so much, Armi. I wish you didn't *have* to get older, but that's life." Wiping away her tears, Delani held Armi at arm's length and gazed at her, trying to memorize every inch of her.

"I'll come tomorrow when you go back to Mrs. Gatoroid's," Delani told her daughter, looking down at her.

The next morning Armi got up early and met her mother in their kitchen corner, where they had a warm cup of tea together. Armi leaned Geddon against the warm pot.

"That pot is not too hot for you, is it, Geddon?" Armi asked her doll with a little smirk.

You know the answer already, Armi. My housing is built with a nano-polymer that repels heat and dirt.

"Isn't this a wonderful morning? We should make time to have tea together more often."

"I would like that too, Mom." Delani reached across the table and squeezed Armi's hand. They smiled at each other as they finished their tea and got up to leave.

They found Conrey already outside his door waiting for them with not quite his normal—at least lately—sad look on his face. There was a little more life to his features today.

"Hey, Conrey, how are you feeling this morning?" Armi asked him, as he gave her a strange look.

"What? You've never asked me that before. Are you feeling ok?"

"Oh, shut up. Let's go. My mom is going with us so she can see our operation for herself," Armi told Conrey, holding Geddon in one arm and puffing her chest out, proud of their recent accomplishments.

"I hope you don't mind, Conrey, but I'm curious as to what you're actually selling." Delani knew Conrey had been hurt emotionally and still needed to heal. She didn't want to hinder his healing in any way, so she spoke gently.

"No problem, Mrs. K'tanhly. it's rather boring anyway, and we could use the company." Conrey continued walking toward the rotunda. Delani just smiled, thinking what a polite, grown-up young Noel-Ni he was.

Like the day before, Mrs. Gatoroid had put the table out, the cups stacked, and the reader ready.

"Good morning, Mrs. Gatoroid," Armi greeted the silver-haired women. She was old—that was evident—but how old, Armi hadn't a clue. She had fine lines around her eyes and mouth, as well as a few age spots on her hands and arms, but not many. She was distinguished-looking, but Armi couldn't figure out why she thought so. She wore the same jumpsuit as everyone else, but on her, it was like a business suit. Armi looked at her mom. "My mom came with us today to see what I've gotten into." Armi smiled at her mother and went over to help Conrey prep the morning drinks.

"They are great kids. You should be very proud of her." Mrs. Gatoroid pointed at Armi as she leaned toward Delani to talk.

"They certainly are, and I *am* very proud of Armi. With Norn gone so much, I would have gone crazy by now without her." Delani felt a little foolish letting a piece of her home life escape and sheepishly turned her eyes downward to avoid looking Mrs. Gatoroid in the face.

"Tut, tut, nothing to be shy about. Torcellans are drawn to each other. We aren't meant to be alone for any length of time. Especially you, with your empathic abilities. I'm surprised you don't tie your husband down, so he doesn't leave." Mrs. Gatoroid knew that Delani worked as a negotiator for the businesses on the station and that her empath abilities made that possible. What most didn't know, including Mrs. Gatoroid was that those abilities were handed down Delani's ancestral line starting with a distant grandfather who was saved by the Empress after she gave him some of her blood.

Delani looked up and smiled at her. "Thank you for that. I miss him dearly, and if I knew it would work, I would definitely tie him down."

Delani was enthralled by the number of customers. She didn't usually read others on the station unless she was negotiating, but she would make an exception since it concerned her daughter. She observed that those purchasing the juice were often somewhat lethargic, but after drinking the juice, they had energy to spare.

Delani walked over to Armi and touched her arm to get her attention.

"Yeah, Mom, what's up? I'm a little busy, ya know." Armi

wasn't trying to be rude, but the line was building, and she was hard-pressed to keep it at a reasonable length.

"I know, dear, but answer me one question." Armi nodded as she continued giving out drinks and making the sales. "Did these customers buy your juice yesterday?" Armi looked at the line and recognized half-a-dozen customers from the day before.

"Yes, there are a lot of repeat buyers. That's good, isn't it?"

Delani lifted her shoulders to indicate she wasn't sure. She had an idea of why they were back but wanted to investigate a little more.

"Mind if I take a cup?" Delani asked Armi.

"Sure, Mom, here ya go." Armi handed a fresh cup to her mom and went right back to handing out purple juice to a small army of yawning Noel-nis.

CHAPTER FIVE

THE ANSWER

Delani didn't waste any time. She took the lift to the floor that was home to the scientific community on the station. She'd done favors for a few of the doctors and wanted to cash one in today.

The sign read, Dr. Flannery, Specialist in Organic Chemistry. The office was pleasantly heated, and there was a scent of flowers in the air. The smell reminded her of running through fields of wildflowers as a child.

"Mrs. K'tanhly, what a pleasant surprise. How may I be of service?" An elderly Torcellan gentleman in a white lab coat greeted her, coming out of the labs in the back.

"Thank you, Dr. Flannery. I could use your expertise on something my daughter has gotten involved with." She held out the cup of juice to the doctor.

"Hmm, isn't your daughter quite young? Seven or eight, isn't she?" the doctor asked with a faint tug at the corner of his mouth.

"Yes, she most certainly is. I'm afraid of what she'll be

doing when she gets a little older." Delani gave the doctor a tired but open smile, saying without words, "My daughter may be the end of me."

"All right, then. What do we have here, and how can I help?"

Delani nodded and began her explanation. "My daughter has combined two different fruits to create this purple juice."

"Leave the sample with me, and I'll run some tests. Come by tomorrow, but not too early. We seniors need our beauty sleep."

Delani chuckled and promised she wouldn't arrive too early.

Delani got the shock of her life that night when Armi told her how much they had made that day.

"You what?" Delani yelled. Armi covered her ears because her mother was so loud.

"Sorry. Sorry, dear. I didn't mean to shout so enthusiastically, but can you blame me? Two thousand credits in a single day?" Delani sat down hard on her makeshift bed and cradled her head in both hands.

"I thought you would be happy about Conrey and I making so much," Armi said, looking confused.

"Dear, it's not that I'm not happy for you, but I think I know why you're selling so much so fast." She took a couple of deep, slow breaths before trying to explain what she surmised to her young daughter. It was easy to see Armi as a lot older than she was, but there was no denying that she was just a seven-year-old girl growing up way too fast.

"The customers just arriving to buy your juice were

tired. I mean *very* tired, lethargic to say the least. Then, after they drank your purple juice, they had an overabundance of energy, and they couldn't wait to get to work."

She paused to gather her thoughts. "Armi, what I'm going to suggest is only an initial theory, but it's a very good one. The chemist I took your juice to this morning agreed with me even before he had any results."

Armi's eyes widened as Delani explained her theory.

"Do you know what a drug addict is?" She looked straight at Armi without flinching when she asked her daughter the question. She wanted Armi to know how important this was. Armi shook her head, then switched to maybe.

"Geddon has taught me all sorts of different things. One time, she mentioned drugs and what the body goes through when deprived of them after having had them for a previous amount of time."

Delani couldn't have been prouder of her daughter at that moment. She nodded. "That's exactly right. The ones who were lethargic this morning drank your juice yesterday. Do you see? They got a boost when they drank it yesterday, and this morning after the boost wore off, they needed another drink to get that boost back." Armi thought about what her mother was telling her, and after a few minutes of juggling the information came up with only one answer.

"I'm a drug dealer, that's what I am." Her daughter's sad look tore a hole in Delani's heart.

"No, no, Armi. You're not a drug dealer—far from it. You're selling a product that others crave. There is nothing wrong with that."

Armi calmed down, and her mother's reasoning helped to alleviate any misgivings she might have had about selling the juice.

"What am I supposed to do? Stop selling it?" Armi looked miserable at that announcement, and Delani didn't have the heart to tell her that was probably the best idea. Instead, she came up with another sensible solution.

"How about we wait until the lab results? If the juice is dangerous to anyone, then you must stop selling it by all means. But if it's *not* harmful, and that the boost is something everyone at the station wants, then keep selling."

CHAPTER SIX

A SOLUTION

Delani read the test report—twice. She just laughed and shook her head. She was shocked and completely caught by surprise as she approached the juice stand. The line wrapped around the rotunda.

"What's going on? I can't believe this line is for the juice," Delani told Mrs. Gatoroid, who just shrugged.

"Mom! Mom, do you have the results?" Worry and fear etched Armi's face.

"Yes, right here." She held up the paper in her hand.

"Well, are you going to tell me?" Armi looked like she was going to explode if she wasn't told something soon.

"It's ok. Nothing toxic, just a slight boost of adrenaline that works its way through the system in a day. Somebody with a bad heart may have problems, but they would be minor." Armi let out a long breath. She had been holding it since she'd seen her mother.

Delani gave Armi a huge grin and an even bigger hug.

"Enjoy the moment, my little girl," she whispered into Armi's ear.

"I will, just as soon as I can take a break!" Armi yelled at her as she dashed back to the table.

CHAPTER SEVEN

DOWNSIDE TO BUSINESS

Delani hung around the fruit and juice stand until the line started to dwindle, about midafternoon. When only a few stragglers were left, a couple of well-dressed and, for the race, very large Noel-nis converged on the juice stand.

"May we have a few words with the proprietor of this establishment?" one of the Noel-ni asked in a disturbing voice.

"Ah... Yeah, just a sec." Conrey told them, then walked the few feet to where Armi and Mrs. Gatoroid were chatting.

"Ah, these dudes want to talk to you, Armi," Conrey told the entrepreneur, jerking his thumb in their direction. Delani had witnessed the whole thing and now walked over to stand in front of the males as Armi, Mrs. Gatoroid, and Conrey arrived.

"What's up, furry and muscled?" Armi asked them. Delani just shook her head and sighed. Conrey and Mrs. Gatoroid were silent and kept their faces blank.

"You're the proprietor?" one of the Noel-nis asked, scrunching his eyebrows in disbelief.

"Yeah. What of it, hair-brain?" Armi was trying to be difficult on purpose. She was good at it, and what were two goons going to do with a seven-year-old, really?

The two Noel-nis laughed. "Well, you are selling an unlicensed product that will require testing and a formal hearing before you are allowed to continue." The one on the left handed Armi a bunch of papers. "Good day to you," he called as they were walking away.

"You have a single eyebrow between you," Armi yelled at their backs. They looked at each other's eyebrows, shrugged, and kept walking. Delani took the papers from Armi and quickly read through them.

"This is bad. They are shutting you down until they deem the juice is ok to drink," Delani announced, looking worriedly at Armi.

"What a bunch of bistok-lovers," Mrs. Gatoroid angrily retorted. Armi shrugged.

"It was great while it lasted." Armi looked at Conrey sadly. There went Conrey's sled. She felt tired all of a sudden.

"Don't worry, dear. I think I have a solution to our troubles." Mrs. Gatoroid had a mischievous grin on her face.

The next morning Armi didn't even want to get out of bed, let alone face Conrey after their problem yesterday.

"Armi, please come out for breakfast. I have something for you from Mrs. Gatoroid," Armi's mother yelled through the door to either wake Armi up or get her to stop moping and come out. With a heavy sigh and even heavier footsteps, she opened her bedroom door and, Geddon in tow, sat down at the kitchen table to face the news.

"How bad is it?" Armi asked her mom, clenching Geddon tighter than she usually did.

"Oh, I don't know. How about you read this and tell me?" Delani placed a credit chit on the table in front of Armi. Delani thought her lips would crack from smiling so widely when she heard Armi gasp and put both her hands over her mouth.

"By the Bitches and the Empress' bistok reserves, this can't be right!" Armi looked open-mouthed at her mother, but Delani just nodded. The amount listed was over twenty-five thousand credits, and it was made out to Armi K'tanhly. There was a note at the bottom from Mrs. Gatoroid.

Armi, you should be very proud of what you have started. I had to pull a few strings, but I got the juice approved. You're a seven-year-old genius, and I envy what you and Conrey have yet to experience. I have deposited the amount listed in your station account and will put all future funds in a similar account in the Federation. Here are a couple of numbers to memorize, and if you ever need to access the funds, just call the bank and give them the numbers. That's it. I'll do the rest. You have made me a rich woman, from a mere forty-percent stake in your juice business. Enjoy life, and get a smile on Conrey's dour countenance somehow. He even irks me.

Mrs. Gatoroid Partner, The Purple Passion Juice Company

THE END

AUTHOR NOTES DOMINIC NOVIELLI

Hello, everyone, and thank you for reading about Armi, her frisky and sometimes funny EI Geddon (who does look a lot like Bethany Anne), and, of course, her faithful companion Conrey. Wow, what an experience this has been! I started writing because of Natale Roberts, who was supportive and determined to get me to write. Well, as you can read, I did. Not just one story, but three. I started out writing about Armi when she was eleven, but kept writing well past the eight-thousand-word mark and went all the way to twenty-six thousand. I eventually cut that down to about twenty-one thousand, but it was still over. I decided to write a different story, focusing on Armi when she was even younger and talking about why she got into so much trouble. Now you see why I went over the eight-thousand-word mark. Armi is a walking case of trouble at every turn.

I have grown to enjoy writing in a very short time, and really don't know what I would do without it. It has become my everything to do every day, and if I don't write at least four thousand words a day, I feel terrible.

I'm here writing these notes and really wondering what to say to you, the fans who have read one of my stories. I have to tell you that I am so excited about this I can hardly sit still enough to type. I want to run outside and shout at the world that they too can read my story—only if they want to, of course. Well, enough about how thankful I am to you for reading and how wonderful it's been to write for Michael and his wonderful world, but I digress. I need to get my four thousand words in today! Keep reading, so people like me have something to look forward to.

Thanks again. I really appreciate every single one of you who have taken time out of your day to enjoy a story of a mischievous child who wants only to help her friend.

Dominic Novielli

HAIKU FROM THE KURTHERIAN UNIVERSE

Barnabas loves chess.
Shinigami always cheats.
He plays with her why?

THE MEDICINE SHOW

LOGAN CAIRD

Magnificent Maxwell's Travelling Medicine Show is coming to town!

Del could not be more excited to see the show, but his family is broke. Since they live on the edge of a city ruined after WWDE they can always dig to find something to trade. Climb a ruined skyscraper, get something valuable, go see the show.

Nothing is ever that simple.

I want to thank both my wonderful parents for supporting all my creative endeavors over the years, my loving girlfriend for telling me more or less daily I need to focus on writing if I want to be an author, and Piper, my adorable (I swear) Doxador lap warmer.

Finally, I want to thank Michael Anderle for creating such a wonderful world and giving so many of us the chance to write in it.

— Logan

THE MEDICINE SHOW

In the Wasteland, Formerly the USA

Delwyn "Del" Winfield leaned out from the side of the building. Holding on with one hand, he watched a caravan of trailers pulled by oxen form a circle outside the city gates. He drew himself back in, foot slipping slightly as he righted himself, and ran through the rubble covering the floor.

A foot hit a loose patch and he slid, slammed into a wall, and fell on his back. His leg slid along an exposed and rusted metal pipe. Blood started soaking his pants, and he called, "Mooooom!" while grabbing his leg.

His mom Alecia jogged up from another room and knelt next to him, saying, "What's wrong, honey?"

Teeth clenched in pain, Del held out his leg and pointed. Holding in tears.

She pulled his pant leg to the side. It was bleeding, but not bad. She pulled out a rag and pressed it to the leg. "Hold it there."

Del pressed the rag to the gash. "Mom! They're here. I saw the Medicine Show."

"That's good, honey," she said, wrapping a spare shirt around his leg to hold the rag in place.

Del's father Sherman stepped into the room. He was holding a white box with an almost circular symbol on it with a bite taken out of it. One side had glass, the other wires. The glass was broken. He said, "What happened, Alecia?"

Alecia replied, "He just got a little excited when he saw the Show setting up."

Sherman grinned and set the box down. "Don't blame him! What're you looking forward to, munchkin?"

"Daad. I'm twelve now. You can't call me munchkin anymore." Del said, frowning at his dad.

"Sorry, kid. Forgot." Sherman said, "Doesn't answer my question, though. What are you most excited about?"

Del winced as Alecia tightened the bandage and said, "I don't know. Maybe the games? Oh! Or the horses. Horses are awesome."

Alecia said, "We *have* horses."

"Guards' horses don't count. These are *Show* horses!"

Alecia flashed a smile and stood up. "Well, if you want to see those show horses we better get back to work. Have to find something worth trading if we want to get into the show."

Del, all gangly limbs, scrambled to his feet and ran off to start searching.

Sherman smiled at Alecia and took her hand. She leaned against his shoulder, squeezed his hand, and kissed his cheek.

Del had always been good at getting into small spaces. Even now that he was as tall as his father, he was still skinny enough to manage places they couldn't fit, which is where he usually found the best stuff.

He climbed on top of a desk and jumped up to grab the edge of a hole, pulling himself up to the next floor. The stairs leading up here had fallen years ago, so this was the only way to get there. The room was dark, most of the light coming up through the hole he'd climbed through.

He moved his feet carefully as he felt his way to the wall. He found something rounded and hard hanging on the wall and brought it back to the light. A red pipe with a handle and some words on it. He dropped it through the hole to the floor below and kept looking.

Going back to the wall, he identified a door a little farther down, but when he pushed it didn't move. The handle turned freely but something on the other side was blocking it, so he sat on the floor in front of the door as his parents had taught him and kicked it. The door barely moved, but sunlight streamed through the crack.

He kicked it several more times, and finally whatever had been blocking it gave way. The door swung open, and there was a *crash* from the other side. The floor beyond the door gave way and slid off the building, plummeting ten stories to the street below. Luckily this section of the city was only frequented by scavengers.

Del crawled to the ledge and looked out across the plains beyond the city to where the Show was setting up. The trailers formed a wall with gaps between them. The people from inside were opening them, setting up barriers to close off the gaps, and assembling the booths.

Outside the circle, a couple of people were moving a booth into place in front of a gate between two trailers. From the ground, no one would be able to see what was going on inside the show without going through the gate.

Two women walked a group of horses between a gap in the trailers. They joked and played around as they led the horses to join the oxen at a river a mile from the Show.

"Was that huge crash you, Del?" Sherman called from below.

Del yelled back, "Sorry, dad!"

"You okay up there, son?"

"Yeah," he said, "Oh! I found something on the wall. I dropped it to your level."

"Fire extinguisher, yeah. It's a bust. The nozzle broke years ago, and whatever was in it leaked out."

"Aww, man," Del said. He pushed himself up and looked around the room he was in. With the door open and light coming through it, he could see that most of this room had already been ransacked. He called down, "I'll keep looking."

Throughout the day Del kept finding reasons to go to the edge of the building and watch the Show set up. Everything he was finding turned out to be a dud. He pulled at a door with a little sign on it, but it was locked.

He felt along the door and tried to sound it out, "Imp loy eees. Oh! Employees Only! *Score.*"

He grabbed the handle and pushed, forgetting he just found it locked. He looked at the walls, but this room didn't have any windows in the hall, so he went to the room next to it and opened that window. Leaning out he looked toward the locked room. Two windows, glass still present, and both of them closed.

He scratched the bandage on his leg. It was starting to itch.

There was no ledge under these windows, so Del went back inside and made his way up to the next floor. Above the locked room was a large, empty room that had once had floor-to-ceiling windows. Now there was just air.

From this side of the building he couldn't see the Show, but he had a good view of the rest of the city. The sun was starting to set, and the line of sunlight was moving across the city.

He untied the end of the rope around his waist, tied it off on a nearby pillar, and lowered himself down to the closed windows below. At first, he was off to the side, but he was able to get to one without much problem.

No seams. The window wasn't designed to open. Most of the windows this high up were not. He braced himself as well as he could and kicked. The glass gave way, and he almost fell into the room. He grabbed the edge as he swung in, cutting his hand on the glass.

He gasped but held on until he stopped swinging. He got his feet under him and untied the rope.

There were several metal shelves against the walls, a table in the middle of the room, and a refrigerator in one corner, as well as cabinets above a counter against one wall. Pressing on his cut hand, he checked the fridge. It was full of food.

All of it had been in the fridge for at least fifty years,

and it hadn't worked in just as long so it was mostly petrified, but it was a good sign.

Del looked through the cabinets and found a metal box with a red plus sign on it. Grinning, he opened it. It was full of bandages and medicine. Most of the medicine would be useless, but the bandages would be worth something.

He looked at his bleeding hand, closed the box, and tore off part of his shirt to bind across his palm. He set the closed box on the table and unlocked the door. It was the kind of door that locked itself each time it closed, so he propped it open with a chair and went to find his parents.

They were two floors down, looking through a pile of rubble. Del told them, "I found a locked room."

Sherman said, "Score!"

Del grinned. "I know!"

Alecia chuckled. "Lead on."

On the way back to the room, Alecia noticed Del's hand and grabbed his wrist. "What happened?"

"Cut it on some glass."

"This is exactly what I said would happen. I did *not* want to come here, because you two are going to get yourselves killed," she fumed as she unwrapped his hand.

She wiped the blood off and cleaned the wound as well as she could before retying it, then offered, "We should just go home."

"No!" Del exclaimed, "Please. Please. Please. Please, Mom. *Please*? I've never seen the Show."

Alecia just rolled her eyes and smiled.

Del grinned. "Thanks, Mom. I'll be more careful, I promise."

"You better. Now, where was that room?"

It took some time for them to make it up two floors to the room. Del was more limber than either of his parents and could climb between the floors more easily. By the time they reached it, the sun had nearly set. He threw open the door with a flourish.

Sherman went straight for the box on the table and opened it. "Full! Nice."

Alecia saw the broken glass and the rope hanging down from above. "You rappelled down the outside? Nicely done."

Del grinned. "I did just like you taught me, Mom."

Sherman sniffed at some of the medicines and frowned. "I don't smell anything. Should smell something, right?"

Alecia checked the same tubes. "Yeah, must have dried out. Worth trading, at least."

She looked over at Del and said, "Why didn't you use one of the band-aids from this emergency kit?"

He scratched his neck. "I didn't want to open the packet. Thought they might not want to trade for it if it was open."

"Oh, honey, come here," she said, taking Del in her arms. "You're more important than whatever we can get for it."

The sun set behind the mountains and the last light faded from the room. The three of them found comfortable places to curl up and went to sleep.

Break Room, Tenth Floor, Early Morning

Del tossed and turned in his sleep, and sweat ran down his neck. He rolled away from his parents, who were huddling together for warmth. He scratched his leg as he woke up. The sun wasn't up yet, but the moon was out, so he could see enough of the room to move around without running into anything.

He put a chunk of rubble in the doorway as he left the room so it wouldn't lock him out and started up to the next floor. His hair was soaked with sweat, and he couldn't stop scratching at his leg.

Climbing up to the next floor was harder than he remembered, but he made it. He bundled up the rope and tied it around his waist, then sat down against the wall. His breathing was fast for such a minor effort.

.The wind blowing across his skin felt nice, so he closed his eyes to rest.

The next thing he was aware of was his mom shaking him awake. The sun still wasn't up, and she had a blanket wrapped around her. "It's freezing up here, Del! What are you doing? Come back down to the room."

He smiled. "I'm fine, Mom." Still covered in sweat, he shivered.

"You're not. Come down, now. I'm not playing around."

"Okay." He got to his feet to follow her downstairs.

She climbed down first, lowering herself through a hole and onto the first stair that was still present. He followed a few moments later, but as he let go of the ledge he wobbled. His vision blurred, and it felt like the building was swaying. He grabbed the railing for support.

His mom turned back from the doorway. "Del?"

"I'm fine, Mom. Just gotta pee."

She rolled her eyes. "Well, hurry up. I don't want you getting sick. It's really cold."

She went back to the break room. Del held the rail until

the world stopped spinning and went to find an out-of-the-way corner. In the moonlight it was harder to see any holes in the floor, so he walked slowly, keeping a hand on the wall as much for balance as to guide him.

He found a small closet. It had long ago been ransacked, but it still had a drain in the floor. He dropped to all fours and threw up on the drain. Kneeling over it, sweat running down his face, he swayed and threw up again.

He lost track of how long he was there, or how many times he threw up. His dad pushed the door open and helped him sit. Sherman said, "You're burning up!" when he touched Del's arm.

He helped Del out of the closet and over into the light. The sun was rising as he leaned Del against the wall and made him sit back down. "Honey! There's something wrong with Del."

Alecia came out of the room and eyed Del. Kneeling in front of him, she pulled the leg of his pants up. Del reflexively scratched the skin around the bandage.

When she removed the bandage, his leg had red spots radiating out from the wound. His skin was sweaty, but he was shivering, and when Alecia touched his leg to clean the blood off, she gasped, "We need to get help. Your leg should not be that hot. Sherman, get that medical kit."

He grabbed the kit from the break room and handed it to her. Del was happy for the breeze through the open window.

Alecia opened one of the packages of antiseptic wipes. It was completely dry, she tossed it aside and tried another. It wasn't until the last package that she found anything worth using. She wiped down his cut as best as she could.

Del didn't even wince when she cleaned the wound, just stared into the distance listlessly.

She put a pad on the wound in his leg and wrapped it with gauze. "Let's go. Help me carry him."

His parents each took one of Del's arms, and they got him to his feet. The world spun around him as he stood, so he leaned on them heavily.

The three of them climbed down several flights of stairs before coming to a floor that didn't have any stairs. Sherman hopped down to the lower floor, and Alecia used the rope to lower Del to him. They had to do that twice more to make it to the ground floor and out of the building.

In the Wasteland, The Medicine Show

The three of them worked their way out of the ruined section of the city and onto the plains. Even from the edge of the city, they could see there was a line of people waiting to get into the show. Above the booth at the entrance hung a large, colorful sign that read, Magnificent Maxwell's Traveling Medicine Show.

A man stood on a stage near the entrance shouting, "Come see the most magnificent show of your life! Come one, come all! See sights that will amaze you! We have jugglers, horse tricks, a doctor to cure what ails you, and strange creatures not seen in these parts for years. Our traders have curiosities lost to time, and a wild man will demonstrate his control over vicious animals. Step right up and experience Magnificent Maxwell's Travelling Medicine Show!"

Alecia was amazed at the speed of his patter. As they

carried Del toward the line, she asked, "Did he even stop to breathe?"

Sherman chuckled, "Didn't sound like it."

They stumbled when Del got dizzy and said, "Can I sit down?"

Alecia said, "I'll stay in line. Take him over there to sit down," pointing to the side of a trailer out of the crowd.

Sherman did just that, and Del slumped down next to the trailer. His dad put a hand on Del's head. "I can't tell if you're getting hotter."

Del smiled up at his dad. "We just walked a mile, Dad."

Nervously Sherman chuckled. "Yeah. Yeah, we did. I'm sure that's it."

Del leaned back. From here he could peek through a crack between the trailer and the metal sheet covering the gap between it and the next trailer. He scratched his arm.

Through the gap, he could barely make out two girls a little older than him standing on the backs of horses. Each straddled two horses as they ran in a large arc, then headed straight toward each other. One of the girls dropped into a split, pushing her horses farther apart, and the other jumped up over her. Her horses ran under the one doing splits, and she landed on them again.

The first girl drew her horses back in and stood, and the crowd cheered. Del smiled. The horses continued to run circles around the clearing, and both girls jumped onto one horse.

Arms locked together, they started flipping from the back of one horse to the next, each swinging the other in wide arcs, as the horses ran. One of the girls grabbed the other by both arms and spun, throwing her partner high in the air.

The entire crowd gasped as she flew. She landed on the back of a horse at a run, hopping to the next horse in line and diving into a flip that put her back on the same horse as her partner.

As he watched, Del's vision blurred. The edges of his sight got dark and pulled in. Within a few moments, he could only see right in front of him. His head slumped to his chest.

Sherman, looking toward the line, didn't notice anything until he heard Del slide down the metal sheeting to the ground. He knelt next to his son and lifted his head, whose eyes fluttered but didn't open.

The red spots had spread up Del's body to his neck. He picked Del up, grunting under the weight, and went to the entrance.

A guard held up a hand as he approached and said, "Tickets please."

Sherman said, "I don't have any." He shifted Del's weight, "Please, I just need to see the doctor. It's my son. I don't know what's wrong."

The guard looked at Del and glanced over his shoulder. At the edge of the crowd, the man who had been shouting about the show was watching them. The guard said, "Look, I'm sorry. I can't. I'll get fired, and this is the only job I've had in a couple months."

Sherman grunted. Del started to slip from his hands, and he shifted him back up against his shoulder. He said, "You're going to let my son die over a job?"

The guard looked at the barker again. At that moment

the person in the front of the line approached Alecia and held out three tickets, saying, "Go."

She thanked him and grabbed the tickets, running up to the entrance. She told the guard, "I've got the tickets!"

The guard said, "Oh, thank god. Please, go right in. The doctor's trailer is in the back on the left." He took the tickets and opened the gate.

Sherman lowered Del's legs to the ground, Alecia put his other arm around her neck, and they headed into the show.

Inside the gate, everything was much louder. A booth just inside offered a chance to throw a knife at a target on a spinning wooden board for "just one ticket." Several people gathered around a table where they were throwing dice at squares, and at another table, someone was moving overturned cups around and asking a local to guess which one had a marble under it.

The three of them ignored all that and headed toward the back of the show. Everywhere they looked someone was trying to get attention. The crowds of locals made it difficult to move, but they were finally able to find the trailer they were looking for.

Tucked away at the back of the show grounds was a trailer with a large metal arm sticking out of the top. The end of the arm had a metal pole sticking into the ground and an ox tied to the pole. On the side of the trailer were painted the words, Dr. Ivo's Tinctures, Treatments, and Cures.

Alecia pulled on the handle to the trailer, but it was locked. She banged on it and called out, "Doctor Ivo! We need your help."

There was no answer. Sherman leaned Del against the trailer while Alecia checked around the side. That side was closed too. She banged on it and called some more.

A young man in a chair near the ox said, "Doc went to get some food. Said he'd be back in an hour."

"Where?" she demanded.

He pointed toward the busiest part of the show.

To Sherman, she said, "Stay here. I'll find him." She jogged off.

Although she wanted to run, there were too many people. She pushed her way through the crowds and eventually found a somewhat clear spot with rows of tables. Fifty or sixty people sat at the tables eating all manner of food, which was being sold at the edge of the area. She stood on the bench at one of the tables and looked around, but she didn't see anyone who looked like her idea of a doctor.

A dozen feet away, a person eating the fried leg of some animal lifted his head and sniffed. His head snapped toward her, and he dropped his food and came over to her. He asked, "Are you okay?"

She said, "No. My son is dying, and I can't find the doctor."

"I'm Doctor Ivo Wahner," he said, sniffing again. "Where is your son?"

"He's back at your trailer. We carried him from the city. Please, I don't know what's wrong with him."

He held out a hand, which she took as she hopped

down from the bench. They pushed their way through the crowd to get back to the doctor's trailer.

Just before they got there, the wind shifted and blew toward them from that direction. Dr. Ivo jerked his head back and ran to the trailer, leaving Alecia behind.

When he got there, he skidded to a stop next to Del and checked him. Hand to the neck, he counted to himself as he looked the boy's body over, pulling aside the sticky and still bloody pant leg. The red spots on Del's leg had merged into one giant red blotch and most of the rest of his body, including his face, was covered in spots.

He said, "His pulse is fast, and he has a fever. Bring him inside." Alecia caught up just in time to hear that. Dr. Ivo unlocked the trailer, and his parents carried Del inside.

Before joining them, Ivo called out to the boy near the ox, "I'm going to need the fan running. Get that ox moving."

The boy stood and whacked the ox, and it started walking in a circle around the pole in the ground. As the pole turned, a wheel at the top moved, which connected to a band that led to another wheel on the top of the trailer. A series of gears operated to a large fan set in the roof of the trailer. As the ox turned the pole, the fan spun up.

Inside the trailer the doctor had them put Del on a reclined chair covered by cracked plastic that crinkled under his weight. He motioned them back and took a jar and a pair of scissors off the counter.

He looked at the parents. "This is a small trailer, and it's already hot in here. Please step outside. I'll do what I can."

Sherman stepped toward the door, but Alecia said, "Can at least one of us stay here?"

"No. I'm sorry, but you will just make it hotter."

Sherman took Alecia's hand, and she reluctantly left the trailer. Dr. Ivo locked the door behind them and set the jar and scissors back on the counter. He opened a cabinet and grabbed a book titled, *Field Guide to Wilderness Medicine*. He sat down and flipped through it.

As he looked through the book, he checked Del over. He leaned close and sniffed his neck, his hand, and then his leg. When he got to the leg, he pulled his pants out of the way and removed the bandage. The wound was festering, almost rotten at the edges and with lines of red radiating across his leg. Nearly the entire leg was red.

He scooped a handful of ground material out of the jar labeled *Aspirin Powder*, mixed it with water from the *Penicillin Tea* jar to make a paste, and applied it to the wound. The fan overhead sucked the strong smells of both the wound and the paste out of the small space.

The doctor washed his hands and looked through the book further. When he came across a section labeled *Septicemia*, with a subtitle of *Blood Poisoning*, he found Del's symptoms.

He checked the paste on the leg. Sniffing at it, he could tell that the worst of the bacteria in the wound was being cleared up. Del didn't look any better, though. He checked the boy's temperature and found it dangerously high. He was still sweating and shivering, and the red spots had merged into blotches across most of his body.

Del's breathing was getting more shallow by the minute. Worse still, his heart rate was increasing, and then dropping so low that Doctor Ivo almost thought he was dead.

He read more of that section of the book and found *Sepsis*, which was the next stage. The words, Possibly fatal jumped out at him, and he growled and put the book away. He got out a scalpel, cut open part of Del's leg near the injury, and then cut his own palm.

The wound on his palm started closing almost immediately, but it was slow enough that he could press it to Del's cut. He let his blood mix with the boy's, cutting his hand a few more times to make sure enough of his blood reached the wound, then sat down to wait.

It wasn't enough. The cut he'd made in Del's leg healed and a small patch of his skin cleared up, but most of his symptoms remained. He stepped to the door of the trailer and leaned out. Spotting both parents a few feet away, he said, "This is going to take all night. I will do everything I can, but you should go find somewhere to rest."

Alecia scrambled to her feet and said, "Can we see him?"

Dr. Ivo hesitated, glancing over his shoulder at Del, then opened the door and motioned them in. "Be quick. He's getting worse, and I don't want to waste any time."

Both parents went to Del's side and took his unresponsive hands. Sherman teared up when he saw how pale his son's face had become between the patches of red. Alecia kissed Del's forehead and whispered, "Don't you dare die. You do not have permission to die, young man."

She rushed out of the trailer, Sherman trying to catch up with her.

Doctor Ivo locked the trailer when Del's parents left and pulled a chair over from a corner next to Del. He dug through a drawer and found a pair of needles, a length of clear tubing, and a roll of medical tape, and sat down in the chair.

He attached the needles to each end of the tube and inserted it into a vein on Del's leg near the wound, taping it in place. Then he did the same in his own arm. Once both needles were in place, he unclipped the tube and let his blood start flowing into the boy.

Every few seconds he clenched his fist to make sure the blood was still flowing. His heart was pumping much more strongly than Del's, and his blood had special characteristics that he knew would help Del heal. He just hoped it would be enough.

He leaned back in the chair and rested his head. "I am not letting you die."

The night passed slowly for Doctor Ivo. He couldn't let himself fall asleep, because he had to make sure to keep his blood flowing. Every thirty seconds for hours on end, he pumped his fist. The blood kept flowing between them.

As the hours passed, Del's wounds closed. The cut on his palm? Gone. The gash in his leg? A faint scar, and then even the scar faded away. As their blood mixed, he stopped sweating so badly. His breathing returned to normal and his body temperature dropped, though not all the way to what was normal for a human.

The red patches covering his body faded. They shrank to nothing, leaving behind unmarred skin. Even a small rug burn Del had forgotten went away. By the time the sun came up the next day, he was in the best health of his life. He woke up a short time after dawn.

He sat up and looked around. "Who are you?"

Doctor Ivo jerked, having fallen partially asleep, and said, "Ivo Wahner. I'm the doctor of the show. Please lie back down."

He stood up and checked Del over. The worst of Del's injuries and the pervasive smell of death were gone. In fact, he could no longer find *any* signs of injury. As he checked the boy over, Doctor Ivo removed the needles from both of them. The needle hole, in each case, closed before more than a few drops of blood dripped out.

"You've made a full recovery. Congratulations."

Del grinned at the doctor. "I feel great! So…uh, can I go now?"

Chuckling, the doctor helped Del down from the table and opened the door of the trailer for him. Del hopped out.

Both his parents, who were sitting on the ground a few feet away, leapt up and ran to hug him. Crushed between them, Del asked in a muffled voice, "Can we go see the horse show now?"

AUTHOR NOTES LOGAN CAIRD

Thank you for reading one of the first, though hopefully not the last, of my writings in the Kurtherian Gambit Universe. I've been telling stories for almost twenty years at this point though most of them have been in the form of Dungeons and Dragons games. Last January, though, my mom died, and it gave me a bit of a shock. Since then I've actively focused on planning a writing career. Life is too short to do anything less than what you love, and I love telling stories.

Writing this story was a bit different than the others I wrote for Fans Write because the POV character changed halfway through outlining it. Originally, Dr. Ivo was going to be the main character in the story. Not only did that change when Del came along, but the entire plot changed! I'm happy with the result, though, because I think this is a better story than would have come from the original idea.

I hope you liked it! I look forward to telling more. If

you liked it enough to want to hear from me, please stop by my site LoganCaird.com and sign up for my mailing list, or follow me on Facebook at Logan Caird. I'll let you know through both of those when I write anything new.

HAIKU FROM THE KURTHERIAN UNIVERSE

ADAM and TOM try
to impart sense to BA
Thankless job, ain't it?

DON'T MESS WITH MINE

BY LISA FRETT

It was a beautiful fall evening in Vermont. That is until she finds out that her man, er, wolf is missing, and an enemy from her past has returned. Well, that's just unacceptable. Now Jenny has to sharpen her fangs and do something about it!

Dedicated to my son Michael, who has to listen to this fangirl's musings.
— Lisa

DON'T MESS WITH MINE

The state of Vermont was, by and large, a beautiful place. For a few weeks during the fall, the mountains exploded with color. As Jenny walked out of her home, she was greeted with the brilliant oranges, reds, yellows, and greens that adorn the trees. Even during twilight, with the sun below the horizon, her vampire eyes could see all the amazing colors of autumn.

Jenny (short for Guinevere) stretched her five-and-a-half-foot-tall, lean, athletic body, working out the kinks of her daytime sleep. She then turned on her tablet to check the news of the day. All the feeds were filled with images of black cargo containers heading into space. This had to be one of the most fantastic things she had ever seen in her centuries of being alive. It was Jen's understanding that this is the doing of the Nacht Bethany Anne and her group. She had to laugh when the cameras focused in on one of the containers where the words, Bite me NASA—Marcus were printed. She didn't know who Marcus was, but he was her hero.

Jen hadn't paid much attention to vampire society and politics since her turning several centuries ago. But Bethany Anne, the "Queen Bitch", had piqued her interest. Before she'd arrived on the scene, Michael had been the head of all things in the UnknownWorld. If you broke Michael's rules, you died. Some might have deserved it, but it was too radical of an approach for Jen.

Jen had her own interests outside of vampire society. She was able to amass a small fortune in the several centuries since her turning. As a female, it was difficult at first.

She stayed with her father, a son of David's, for several decades after becoming a vampire. Unlike David, who was a complete asshole, her father was kind to her. He saw to it that she had everything she could ever need and taught her how to be independent and take care of herself. Some of what he taught her was business and martial skills. Her favorite lessons were hand to hand combat. But she became very proficient in business and swordsmanship as well.

Unfortunately, Jenny didn't get along well with the other vampires in the house. A couple of her brothers didn't believe that her lessons were appropriate for women. Jenny disagreed. She was always getting into alter-cations because of it. It became so bad that she and her father thought it would be best if she left.

Her father made certain she would be well taken care of. He opened several bank accounts for her under male aliases. If it was ever necessary for someone to be present at the bank, she had a trusted friend that would show up as her proxy.

Shortly after arriving in the Americas, Jenny began investing in businesses and property. She used a proxy up until the beginning of the twentieth century, when it became a little easier for women to be actively involved in business.

Knowing that there really were things out there that went "bump" in the night, she'd kept up with her dad's lessons. She continued training and practicing for any incident that might occur.

Jenny liked to train in her everyday clothes. Her rationale was to get used to fighting in what she would be wearing if she ever had to defend herself. Today she was in her comfortable jeans, a white tank top, and a black leather jacket. Her long brown hair was in a ponytail, and she had on her favorite New Balance running shoes. On her one hundred-plus acre property, she had laid out several obstacle courses. After a quick stretch, Jen took off for the closest one.

The first obstacle was a ten-foot wall. She easily grabbed the top and pulled herself up and over using her upper body strength. From the top of the wall, she jumped to the ground and landed in a forward safety roll. Next was a series of varied-height vaulting stones, followed by a railing that she jumped onto and balanced the length of.

When she reached the middle of the railing, she sensed someone to her right and recognized the energy of the person running toward her. A disheveled young girl around nine years old bounded into her and knocked her off the beam.

"Sammy! What the hell?!" Jenny exclaimed.

Glancing at the young girl, she said, "You look awful. Are you OK?"

Sammy was her neighbors' foster daughter. Jen's neighbor Dan could have passed for a male model. Jen thought of him as beefcake. *Her* beefcake, since they had been a couple for several decades. Dan and Sammy were werewolves, and they'd separated from the North American pack so that he could be with her. Jen had been upset when she'd initially heard that they left but had been selfishly happy they had. She couldn't imagine her life without those two.

They lived separately, since Dan worked out of the house during the day when Jenny slept. He knew it wasn't necessary to have separate homes, but he kept his office at his property so there wouldn't be a chance to bother Jen, and out of respect for her. It was very thoughtful of him, but she really wished he would be there when she woke up.

Jenny gave Sammy a serious once-over. Something bad must have happened.

Looking at the young girl she saw that she was covered in dirt. She had on canvas tennis shoes with sparkle designs, jeans, and a blue unicorn tee shirt with a torn flannel shirt over it. She had tear tracks smeared on her face where she had obviously been crying. And was that blood? Who did Jen have to beat up? The poor girl must have run all the way from her house. Where was Dan? He should have been there with her. Jen didn't know what had happened but whoever had done this to Sammy was going to pay—most likely with their life.

"You have to get them, Aunt Jenny!" Sammy always

called Jenny her aunt or auntie. "They broke into our home and took Daddy. They said he had something they wanted. Daddy wouldn't give it to them, so they shot him in his legs and dragged him away. I tried to stop them, but they kept pushing me off. I sneaked away when they weren't looking and hid. They took him!" Sammy started to cry again.

Jenny pulled Sammy into her arms and hugged her close. "I'll take care of this. Tell me who 'they' are?"

"I think it's the Renegade werewolves auntie. I recognized one of them." She wiped a tear away. "Someone kept saying that the 'boss will be mad if they don't find it.'"

Jen nodded, giving thought to what Sammy was telling her. The Renegades weren't really a pack, they were an illegal group of werewolves that had either been kicked out of the North American pack or had left because of irreconcilable differences. As an afterthought, Jen asked, "Do you know what 'it' is?"

"No. But Liam, a guy who works with daddy, came by the other day with a case that had a bunch of bottles in it. He said that what was in the bottles could eat stuff or something. I don't know what they were talking about, but he seemed really excited. They went into Daddy's office to talk and closed the door, so I couldn't hear what they were talking about."

Normally, a werewolf like Sammy would be able to hear through a closed door, but Dan had built his office with that in mind. He had soundproofed it so visitors to his home wouldn't be able to listen in if he had business to handle.

"Let's go to your house and see if we can find some clues as to where they might have taken your dad, and what they are looking for. I've got to head into the house and get a few things first."

In the basement of her home, Jen placed her hand on a part of the cement wall that looked a little worn. She needed to fix that. An observant person would notice it.

She pressed the worn spot and pulled back a piece of the wall, which opened into a room filled with gear of all kinds. One wall held shelves containing different kinds of handguns, shotguns, and rifles. Her bugout bags were on the ground in front of them. Another wall held swords, knives, and other martial weapons. A third wall had a rack of tactical clothing and armor.

She put on black tactical pants, a black shirt, and combat boots. A black nylon duty belt supported a combat knife (silver-plated for good measure), two holsters for her Colt 1911 Government model .45s, and several pouches filled with loaded magazines for the Colts.

She looked at her sword collection and chose a katana that her father gifted her. The blade was silver-plated. Her dad expected that she would have to fight off vampires and werebeasts throughout her life. He wanted her to be prepared. She placed it in a sheath with a shoulder strap.

In the event she came across a vampire or werewolf, Jen threw some extra magazines with silver frangible bullets into the thigh pockets of her cargo pants. She also had two pair of silver-plated handcuffs, a couple rolls of duct tape (every bugout bag needs duct tape), and a silver chain for good measure. She placed the items in one of her backpacks and went back upstairs.

Jen and Sammy climbed into Jen's SUV, a black Range Rover Sport SVR with dark-tinted windows, and headed to Dan's and Sammy's house.

Dan's two-story farmhouse was at the end of a long gravel driveway. Jen exited the vehicle, checked her.45s and slung her katana's sheath over her shoulder. Last she put on her backpack. She turned to Sammy, "Stay in the SUV while I check out the house. Keep the doors locked."

The young girl nodded.

Jen examined her surroundings but didn't notice anything out of the ordinary. Three stairs led up to the front porch, where two wood Adirondack chairs flanked a picture window beside the front door.

Not knowing what to expect, she cautiously walked up the steps and slowly opened the door. Once inside, she knew that she wasn't alone. She could hear movement. Jen drew one of her .45s.

Vampires' senses were more enhanced than humans' and Jen put them to use. She listened carefully, there was movement in the basement. When she got closer she sniffed. She thought she could smell dog. *No*, she thought, *not a dog, werewolf*. She sniffed again. It's not Dan. They smell different. She quietly removed her backpack and placed it on the floor.

Knowing that there was a Were in the basement, Jen didn't feel the need to be silent anymore. If she could hear and smell him, then he could definitely hear and smell her.

"You can make it easier on both of us if you come upstairs now. I just want to talk to you," she yelled

A gravelly male voice laughed below and said, "You have no idea what you are up against, little woman."

She just rolled her eyes. When it came to chest-beating and testosterone-filled rants, Weres were some of the worst, whether in human or animal form. It didn't bother her. She'd never met a werewolf she couldn't take in a fair fight.

She heard someone coming up the stairs. She saw a burly man dressed in the flannel shirt, jeans, and mud boots that were standard Vermont attire year-round.

He looked her over. "You really *are* a little lady." He sniffed the air. "Oh! This is too good! You're a vamp. Little bloodsucker, you're out of your league, and you're about to die."

"And you're a comedian." Jen brought up her .45 and blew out both of the Were's kneecaps. She chuckled. "See? This *is* funny."

He collapsed and thrashed around on the ground. "You fucking bitch! That fucking *hurts*!"

Jen shot him in the gut. "Keep talking, Fido. I can do this all day."

She knelt and put her face near the Were's neck. "Now, you're going to tell me where you took the man who lives here." She pulled back briefly and he saw her glowing red eyes and fangs. "Or you're going to be dinner. Make that breakfast, since I just woke up."

"Bitch!" He was hurting, and the silver of the bullets was keeping him from healing fast, but he still tried to stand. That is until he realized that there a knife strategically placed below his stomach near his favorite body part.

"You will tell me, or you will lose your favorite play toy."

Not wanting to lose his man-, err, wolfhood, he quietly obliged. "Yeah. OK. They're in a house near the border, close to Newport. I'll give you the address. Just please, don't…do that to me."

Jenny's eyes were still glowing red. "We'll see." She really didn't want to kill him. But he didn't need to know that.

She removed a pair of silver chains and some duct tape from her backpack.

Jen had the Were turn onto his stomach. She wrapped duct tape around his wrists. She then placed a pair of her silver-plated handcuffs over the tape. The cuffs were designed to hold against a werewolf's strength, the tape should keep the silver from burning the werewolf's flesh.

"You can try and get out of these, but I doubt you'll succeed. Those handcuffs are silver. Fighting against them will, most likely, cause them to come in contact with your skin. I'm pretty sure that will ruin your night."

"It's all good. I promise, no fighting. I don't want to die, or…" Fido paused.

"Or lose your little friends." Jenny grinned as she finished the statement for him.

He grimaced. "Right."

She turned back to Fido. "Now, let's finish this…" She got to work securing him.

Before leaving, Jen admired her handiwork. It was good, if she did say so herself. In the middle of the basement floor was a werewolf in human form sitting in a chair. His hands were cuffed behind his back. Excluding his head, he had been thoroughly secured to the chair with duct tape. He wasn't going anywhere. His mouth had a clean cloth stuffed inside and secured by duct tape. For good measure, she took her silver chains and wrapped them around the werewolf and further anchor him to the chair.

"I'm sure you understand that I can't have you leave to warn your pack that I'm on the way."

He made a "Mmphft" sound.

Before leaving, Jen made a quick sweep of the house for any sign of the bottles with the mystery substance, but she couldn't find anything odd or out of place. Except, of course, the werewolf duct-taped and chained in the basement.

She hopped in her Range Rover and took Sammy to Rogan's house. Rogan was an old friend of both Jen's and Dan's. Sammy always enjoyed visiting Rogan, and she felt very comfortable leaving Sammy with him.

Jen put the address given to her by the werewolf into her phone and headed for the house. Sure, she would incur international roaming charges by keeping her phone on, but she could afford the cost.

Vermont has a lot of long, winding, graveled dirt driveways, and this one was no exception. Unfortunately for Jenny, this one had several guards alongside it. She couldn't see them, but she could "feel" them. Because of this, she parked her SUV on the side of the road and exited the vehicle before the driveway.

In the back of her Range Rover, Jen had a hidden and locked compartment where she kept a few extra items, including body armor and gloves. Once she'd armored up, she slung her katana over her right shoulder. She didn't want to take any chances, not when she was walking into a Were den.

When Jen sniffed the air, she could smell a Were in wolf form a short distance ahead of her. She knew he could smell her too, so there would be no element of surprise. Her best bet was to get to him before he raised the alarm. Which, for a wolf meant she had to keep him from running. It probably wouldn't be too big a problem though since most Weres felt like they had something to prove. So, Jen appealed to the Were's nature, and straight-up challenged him.

"Hey, dog breath, have you ever had your ass kicked by a girl?"

Jen heard a growl, then saw movement a little to her right. She heard the leaves crunch under the wolf's paws as he leapt toward her. She did a run and slide under him like she was stealing home plate, grabbed his right rear paw, and pulled as hard as she could. The speed and force of this action ripped the leg off the wolf's body, and he landed in a bloody heap and began changing back to his human form.

Jen looked down at the one-legged naked man writhing on the ground before her. She could see that the wound was already starting to close. She glanced at the leg she still held in her hand.

"Now," Jen said to him, "you have a very good friend of mine locked up in that house. You're going to tell me exactly where he is, or I'm going to shove this leg so far down your throat it's going to come out your ass."

"I don't know," Dog Breath answered. "I *don't* know," he reiterated. "He's up at the main house, but I don't spend much time there. Only high-ranking Weres get to go in the main house. Damn!" He growled. "This fucking hurts! Bitch!" She watched him wince in agony as he clutched his stump.

"Oh, stop whining. It will grow back you, big baby. Why'd they kidnap him? What do they want from him?" Jen pressed.

He growled "I think... I think I heard Woddin say something about your boyfriend's company creating a powder that can corrode most metals, including silver. Woddin wants it."

"Huh." Jen thought about it. "He probably wants to try and get back at the North American Pack Council."

Jen tossed the wolf's leg on the ground and took off toward the house. As certain as she was that they would keep Dan alive, she was equally certain that they would hurt him until he gave them what they wanted. And once they got what they wanted, there would no longer be a reason to keep him alive. Woddin was a dead wolf. Of that she was positive.

She quickly ran up the road. To a human's eyes, she would have looked like a blur.

Jen could move even faster than most. Because of all the practicing she'd done, she'd learned to feel an "energy," for lack of a better word. She used this energy to help her with some activities, and running was one of them. She didn't tap into it too much though. Although it gave her a boost during the activity, it drained her strength quicker. She'd heard that members of Bethany Anne's team sometimes carried bags of blood with them on missions. Jenny thought that maybe she could start carrying coolers with bagged blood in her vehicle when she went on adventures like this.

Jenny had to focus on getting to Dan. She was focusing so hard that she lost situational awareness. Even moving as fast as she was, a werewolf guard was able to time his leap just right. He knocked her on her butt and got in a good bite on her left arm.

She tried to fight off the wolf, but his jaw was clamped down so tight that, try as she might, she couldn't shake him off. Razor sharp teeth were biting into her arm. It hurt like hell.

Jen grabbed the holstered Colt 1911 on her right side and shot the wolf point-blank in the head. Blood, bone, and brain matter flew everywhere. She looked down. Was that an eyeball on her chest?

Jenny jumped up and brushed the eyeball off her. "EWW! EWW! EWW!" The wolf's torso was lying headless nearby. She shot at the torso of the wolf. "That was nasty! Eww!" She holstered her gun and took back off running up the road.

Ahead, there were three Weres in human form. She plowed into one of them, knocking him on the ground. Quickly, Jen drew her katana from its sheath and sliced his head off.

She turned to face the two remaining men. One of the men drew a pistol and shot at her. She moved quickly, but not fast enough, and the bullet grazed her left arm—the same arm that Dog Breath had chewed on earlier.

The third guy dove for her legs and tackled her to the ground. Now she was pissed. She punched the face of the guy hugging her legs, loosening his grip. His left ear was beautifully exposed. She pulled her knife from her belt and shoved the blade through his left ear until it came out his right. Jenny felt confident that he was no longer a threat.

The one man still standing aimed again, this time at her head. Jen quickly rolled to her side to avoid the bullet, but the shithead kept shooting. She did a quick somersault toward his unarmed side, stood up and hit the back of his head with the butt of her knife. With him off balance now, Jen spun and gave him a sharp kick in the butt. The kick was so powerful that he dropped his gun—and his face— onto the gravel of the road.

Jen picked up his gun, knelt beside his head, and proceeded to grind his face into the gravel. She was pretty sure he tried to say something, but with all the dirt and rocks in his mouth, all she heard was something along the lines of, "Grmfpht." She wasn't sure what grmfpht meant, but she was fairly certain it wasn't nice.

With shithead's gun, she shot the two men in both kneecaps. Werewolves healed quickly, but she hoped that this would slow them down long enough for her to kill Woddin and free Dan.

Before now, the only member of the Renegade pack that Jen'd had contact with was Woddin, the Alpha. The Renegade pack wasn't located in Vermont, or at least they hadn't been in the past. Woddin, however, had come to Vermont before.

Woddin had arrived a short time after he was kicked out of the North American Pack Council. She wasn't sure why he had been kicked out. Probably because he was a murderous psychopath, but that was just a guess. He had gone on a feeding frenzy after he first got to Vermont, and the council had sent Dan and a couple others to take care of him. That was when Jenny had first met Dan. Jenny, Dan, and the gang had found Woddin. A fight ensued, and they had been able to beat Woddin down enough to wear him out. Unfortunately, he still had enough energy to run away before they could detain or kill him. After leaving Vermont, he stayed below the radar so as not to bring attention to himself. Apparently, he had been busy building an illegal pack of his own filled with those who left the council—the Renegades. Well, now Woddin was back, and he had an agenda.

There was a clearing between the tree line and the house where Dan was being held. A small porch led up to the home, and on each side of the door was a guard. She wasn't sure if she wanted to try a frontal assault, or if she could find an unguarded entrance somewhere else. Slipping back into the woods, she looked for another way to enter.

Well, that's convenient, she thought. There was an unguarded cellar door on the side of the house. She listened for movements but didn't hear anything. She didn't smell anything either, so she cautiously made her way to the entry.

When she got to the door, she could see a possible reason it was unguarded, although she felt it was rather shortsighted of the Weres. The door had a massive padlock. Understanding that the Renegades had just taken this property over, Jen guessed they hadn't had time to put in more secure hardware.

Hoping that this wasn't one of those "too good to be true" moments, Jen took a chance and brought out her Leatherman. Opening the Phillips screwdriver, she began unscrewing the latch from the door. Once the latch had been removed, she carefully opened the door and crept down into the basement. Talk about a lesson in futility.

At the bottom of the steps, Jen threw her hands up and shouted, "OK, guys. You know I'm here. I know you know I'm here. Let's just finish this. Where's Dan?"

The room quickly filled with men. Some of the men began to change into their wolf forms. *Well, fuck!* she thought. *In for a penny. In for a pound.* With that, she ran towards the waiting pack.

The space was relatively small, dark, and full of humans and werewolves. Literally backing into a corner to control the angle from which the enemy could come at her, Jen dropped into a fighting stance and prepared for the onslaught.

The first to come at her was a human male a tad shorter than her. She did a roundhouse kick to his knee, then came around with a solid kick to his face, knocking him down. When he fell his head bounced off of the hard floor, knocking him unconscious.

The guy next to him tried taking advantage of the exposure from her kick and struck at her with his fist, but Jen deftly ducked out of his fist's path. This put her in perfect position to send a powerful snap-kick to the man's groin, and he doubled over in pain. Jenny rolled over his back and kicked the two behind him. One of the men fell from the force of the kick. She stomp-kicked his face, crushing it. The other remained standing but was very wobbly. She punched him in the face and broke his nose, and he fell to the floor crying. She turned back to the man that was still doubled-over and gave him a hard side-kick to his butt causing him to go head first into the cellar wall. He fell to the floor unconscious.

Jen told the crying man on the floor, "That's pathetic, dude. Grow a pair." She stomp-kicked his knees causing him to scream in agony. "Don't get up!"

Next came a pair of wolves. They prowled up to her, snarling. She had to admit they were big ones. The one to the right was drooling, and she said, "Ugh. You're drooling. That is disgusting!" The wolf lunged at her, and to cut the distance and to give her a little more power, Jen launched a spinning hook-kick into the wolf's jaw. She heard the crack of the bone breaking as she hit it. This also put her in the perfect position for an axe kick to the head of the other wolf. Because werewolves healed quickly, she wanted to make certain they didn't get up. She quickly drew her katana and sliced their heads off.

Only one wolf and two humans remained. The humans pulled out pistols, and the wolf waited for the two to shoot before making his move. Jen rushed the man on the right. She dropped her sword and grabbed his gun hand before he could get a shot off, pointed the gun at the other man and pulled the trigger. The bullet hit the guy in the gut, and he fell to the ground in agony. Yanking the gun free, she shot the man she held in the head. That just left the wolf.

Seeing that his partners were incapacitated, or dead, the

last wolf lunged at Jenny, knocking her down. She didn't want to get into a grappling match with a wolf, but she really didn't have a choice.

The wolf stood over her with his giant paws on either side of her head and tried to bite her, but somehow she found the strength to hold him back.

Managing with one hand to keep the wolf's jaws from closing on her face, Jen looked to her right and saw the hilt of her sword. In a quick movement, Jenny grabbed the wolf's right paw with her free hand. She pulled the paw across her body while pushing his head away from her. She turned a little to the left and pushed her butt out from under the weight of the wolf. Jenny scrambled to her sword snatched the hilt and sliced through his neck, doing away with the final danger in the room.

She knew Woddin was still somewhere in the house. The pack beta was most likely with him since she didn't think any of these were the beta.

She cleaned the blood and guts off her sword with the shirt of one of the incapacitated men and gently placed the katana back into its sheath. She turned to those still living and shot each in the kneecaps so they wouldn't bother her while she was dealing with their boss.

Jenny wanted to be certain she had enough energy to go after the rest of the Weres in the house, so she extended her fangs and bit into one of the dead wolves. Once her energy was restored, she continued searching the house.

The rest of the basement was clear, so she went up the stairs. At the top of the steps, she was greeted by a man she had seriously hoped to never see again. She had to admit, for an evil demon-spawn puke-bucket he was handsome in his worn jeans, red and black flannel shirt, and hiking boots. He was well-built with black hair and dark eyes. Unfortunately, his crappy personality outweighed his physical appearance.

Behind and to the right of him stood a twentyish woman. She was wearing a dark, loose tunic shirt, a pair of gray leggings with little puppy heads, and gray pumps. On a farm. In Vermont. "Definitely not a local," Jen thought.

Jen's eyes glowed red, and fangs protruded, she looked at the man. "Woddin, you festering piece of horseshit! What did you do with Dan? Why are you doing this? Was it really worth all the dead and injured?"

Woddin's big chest rumbled a low laugh. "Collateral damage."

"What do you know about your boyfriend's company?" he asked her.

"Because of you, there are a bunch of dead and injured in the basement and outside. I don't want to talk. I want to know where Dan is."

Woddin grinned, and his girlfriend gave an annoying giggle. "How about this?" he said. "You have a few minutes to save your boy toy before the bomb goes off."

With that, Woddin threw an object that emitted some kind of smoke. It didn't seem toxic, but Jen didn't really want to test it. Woddin and his girlfriend ran out of the room in a hurry. Jen just wanted to free her boyfriend before they both became puddles of goo from an exploding bomb.

Jenny tried to calm herself. With the exception of visibility, the smoke in the room wasn't bothering her too much. She picked up Dan's scent in an upstairs room and found the stairs off to the right.

When she got to the top of the steps, Dan's scent was much stronger. Following it, she found a locked door. With a swift kick, Jen shattered the door handle and surrounding wood.

The room was sparsely furnished. There was a double bed against the far wall, a dresser, and two wooden chairs. Dan hung from the ceiling by the rope around his hands.

Not knowing how much time they had before the alleged bomb blew, she swiftly drew her katana and sliced through the ropes above his hands.

She caught Dan as he fell and then sheathed her katana. Not wanting to take a chance with a possible bomb, Jen threw Dan over her shoulder in a fireman's carry and jumped through the window.

She gently set him on the ground and examined his muscled torso for any injuries the pack might have inflicted. Looking around, she found a nearby tree to sit Dan up against.

"I thought our date wasn't until tomorrow night, but this was fun. You really do know how to show me a good time." Jen smiled as she looked into his dark eyes.

"I know how much you like a little maiming." Dan looked around. He could see a couple of bodies just inside the woods. At least one looked dead. The others looked alive and were probably healing. He grinned at her. God, he loved her. He was glad she had come for him.

Jenny untied the rope around his hands. "They mentioned a bomb. I'm thinking we don't want to stick around here."

"So *that's* why we flew through the window."

She smiled. "I wanted to sweep you off your feet."

Dan laughed. "Corny, but effective. You definitely succeeded." He gave her a smile that melted her insides. "Let's go."

As they were walking down the driveway, the house exploded behind them. They sped up to try to outrun the falling debris.

Jen swerved around a sofa that landed in front of her. "Damn! How big was that bomb? There were still Renegades alive in the basement. I shot them in the kneecaps so they wouldn't get in my way."

Dodging a wooden plank that flew at him, Dan replied, "Well, they're dead now. I'm fairly certain nobody in the house survived that blast, including the ones in the basement."

"That fuckwad killed his own men! What a fucking asshole."

When they made it back to the SUV, Jen returned her armor and gloves to the container she'd pulled them from and climbed into the driver's seat.

Turning to Dan, Jen asked, "Are you really all right? He didn't hurt you?"

Dan grinned at her. "Only my pride. Being saved by a beautiful woman makes it easier to bear."

Jenny punched him hard in the arm.

"*Ouch*! What the hell was that for?" Dan asked.

"For scaring Sammy and me. She told me who had you, and. I thought the worst. And now that jackhat is loose again. Fuck. I'm mad."

He smiled. "Sorry to scare you."

Jen sighed. "Don't be an ass." She smiled then. "I'm glad you are OK. What's this all about, Dan? I thought Woddin was gone. I know about the powder. I managed to get one of the pack members to tell me. But what do they want with it? Is there some way of using it that could benefit wolves?"

"Actually," Dan answered, "yes, there is."

As Jen drove to Rogan's house Dan continued, "First, understand that this corrosive powder is able to weaken every metal we've tried it on. That includes iron, steel, copper, gold," he paused and looked at her, "and silver."

Jen's face turned white. "Silver? Holy shit, Dan. That could be bad for the UnknownWorlders."

Dan sighed. "I know." He paused as he thought about it. "There's more. We found that if we coat an object with the powder like, say, clothing, and if a silver frangible bullet comes in contact with the material, it transforms and weakens the metal enough to change its effect on the individual shot, and all it takes is a minute amount. The change to the metal causes the bullet to lose some of its penetration ability, and the change to the silver is enough where the injury isn't quite as bad. That's why Woddin and his pack wanted it. Imagine if the Weres you cut through today had clothing and fur coated in this powder. With the exception of those whose heads you cut off, your silver bullets would have had much less of an effect on them. Even the lead in regular bullets would have been affected. If your sword had come in contact with any of the material, you might have been successful in slicing off a limb before your sword broke. But it *would* break. At least, that was what happened when we did the testing."

She pulled the Range Rover to a stop in Rogan's drive and looked at Dan. "First, if Woddin or any of his pack broke my sword using this stuff, I would have crushed his skull so flat his eyes would be looking out the back of his head. Second, you would be on my shit list for the next decade."

Dan looked at her. "*Me?* Why me?"

"Because your company made the stuff. So, by association, *you!*" she said emphatically.

He raised an eyebrow at her.

She harrumphed and stuck her tongue out at him.

Before opening the door to exit the SUV Dan asked, "Why didn't you kill the bastard before freeing me?"

"Trust me," Jen answered, "I want him dead, and I plan on making that happen. But he mentioned the bomb, and I didn't know how long I had. I honestly think he would have blown it with him in the building if he killed us along with him. I wanted you...us...safe. I can always track him down and kill him later. Which I will.

"Let's go see Sammy. She'll want to know you are OK. She was terrified for you." Jen opened her door and headed for the porch.

Dan, Jenny, and Sammy were in Dan's kitchen relaxing. Jenny was catching Dan up on the events of the evening. Sammy was having a late-night snack of chocolate chip cookies and milk before they sent her to bed. Dan was famished. He hadn't eaten for almost a full day. He made a couple of burgers and a bunch of fries for himself, and a burger and a salad for Jen.

Since Sammy felt comfortable and safe in the house once again, they put her to bed. With Jen on one side and Dan on the other, they carefully tucked her into her unicorn and rainbow comforter. Sammy wanted to tell them that they'd tucked her in so tightly that she couldn't move, but after giving it more thought, she *did* feel more secure. Both Jen and Dan kissed her on her forehead and wished her a good night.

In his office, Dan went to the bookcase and pulled out a book, and a section of the wall opened to reveal a closet.

Jen leaned against his desk with her arms crossed on her chest. "That's kind of cliché, don't you think?"

Dan grinned and gave her a wink. "It worked, didn't it?"

Jen just smiled at him, and he walked into the closet.

"I want to be certain that they didn't find the case with the bottles. After Barry dropped it off, I locked it in here." He took a gray equipment case off a chest-high shelf, walked back to his desk, and placed it on the top. Once he put his thumbprint into a biometric reader, two latches on the case clicked.

Dan opened it and looked inside. "Well, fuck," he exclaimed.

Jen looked into the case. The hard foam material inside had custom indents for bottles, and several held dark brown bottles that appeared to be filled with a powdery substance. One indent was empty.

Jen looked from the case to Dan. "Let me guess…one's missing?"

Dan's dark brown eyes locked on hers. "We're screwed."

Jen smiled at him. "Well, that's rather defeatist of you."

Dan looked at her thoughtfully. "You want to go hunting, don't you?"

"You *so* get me," she said. "When's the last time you got to hunt? I mean, *really* hunt? Do you think Woddin has it?"

Dan did love it when they hunted together. Jen was hot when she got her mad on, and when she got all vampy, well… "What are we waiting for? Let's go!" he replied enthusiastically. "I can smell Woddin's wolf scent in the house. I thought it might have been from when he captured me earlier, but the Were you taped into the chair downstairs got free. It looks like he had help, so I'd bet that Woddin came back."

It took just a minute for Dan to change into his wolf. Dan was a big wolf. His fur was dark gray with black tips, shading to brown toward his stomach and around his ears. He had brilliant gray eyes. Dan's wolf took Jen's breath away, he was so beautiful. At least, *she* thought so.

While Dan was changing, Jen called Rogan to see if he could stay with Sammy while they were out. As always, Rogan was more than happy to help. They waited for him to arrive, then Jen and Dan went outside and picked up the werewolves' scents.

"It smells like they both left in wolf form," Jen said as she sniffed the air. She smiled. "It's a good night for a run." Dan howled.

The scent took them to one of the numerous rundown abandoned barns that dotted the nearby countryside. Jen heard sounds coming from inside. Woddin, back in human form, stepped out of the front door.

Smiling, he said, "You found me. Good. This will end quickly, then."

Dan growled, and Jen said, "You have our bottle. We want it back."

Woddin looked at her and laughed. "Just like that, huh? I don't think so."

In true Jen fashion, she drew her weapon and shot Woddin in the gut. "That was a silver bullet, in case you're wondering."

Woddin held his stomach as if in pain, then he pulled his hand away and smiled. They could see his wound already healing. The silver didn't appear to have any effect.

He looked at her. "Well, the stuff worked." He looked at Dan "Nice. Thanks for that."

Still looking at Dan, he said, "It looks like we'll have to do this the old-fashioned way."

Soon there was a light gray, almost white wolf with dark, brooding eyes standing before them. Woddin's wolf was taller, but Dan's wolf was sturdier.

Jen thought it would be a good fight, but unfortunately, she wasn't going to get to watch. Behind her was the same female who had been with Woddin earlier that evening, and she was holding the missing jar. Jen's eyes glowed red as she turned and looked at the girl. She gave her a big fangy grin, and said, "Boo!"

The girl's eyes turned to saucers, and she dropped the jar and ran as fast as she could. Since she was still wearing the pumps, she fell a lot. Jen just shook her head. Thankfully the jar hadn't broken when it fell. She turned back to the dogfight.

Both wolves' hackles were raised. Woddin charged, but Dan jumped into the air and came down on top of him. Dan tried to bite Woddin's flank, but Woddin dodged to the side, avoiding major injury.

Teeth bared, they attacked each other. The sight was mesmerizing, yet horrific. Teeth and claws were everywhere. One moment Dan was on top with Woddin at the bottom, and the next it was the other way around. Both wolves had injuries.

Jen really wanted to step in to help Dan, and she would have if she'd thought that Dan would lose. But this was a dominance thing. She just needed to let Dan do this. Damn, she really wanted to kick Woddin in the face. She'd feel much better for it.

Watching the wolves fight was like watching an old cartoon where the fighters were engulfed in a dust ball with the occasional arm or leg sticking out. If it hadn't been Dan in there, she'd have thought it was pretty comical.

For a while there it looked like Woddin was going to come out on top. She was sort of cheering for that because then she'd get to kick his head in. A moment later Dan rammed his shoulder into Woddin's midsection. It was such a hard hit that Woddin ended up against a sturdy maple tree.

Dan stood over Woddin's prone body. He didn't want to give him any more chances. With one bite, he ripped out Woddin's throat.

Blood and gore were everywhere, but it was over. They

had the bottle with the corrosive powder, and Woddin was no more.

Jen feared what the jar's contents could be used for. Woddin'd had an unknown benefactor, but the powder was safe for now. Personally, Jen liked her bladed weapons. She would be really upset if they were rendered useless, but for now, it was all good.

She looked at Woddin's lifeless body, then she looked at *her* wolf. Scratching Dan behind the ears, she said to him, "Let's go home, hon. I think we've earned our peace for one night."

FINIS

If you're reading this, then I hope that means you read through the story and hopefully enjoyed it.

As a professional geek (System Administrator by day), I do write a lot. But usually, it's tech manuals and how-to manuals for end users. So, when Michael Anderle opened his universe for his fans to write fan-fic in, I thought it might be fun. I'm a big fan of the universe and had a lot of fun dreaming up Jen and Dan. I also think that Sammy can be fun to look into as well. But I have to let her grow up a bit.

Anyway. Thank you.

HAIKU FROM THE KURTHERIAN UNIVERSE

Wrinkle-assed ball-sack,
Llama-sniffing fudge packer.
Who thought of those, Mike?

SPIRIT WHISPERER

BY S.E. WEIR

Claire has known all her life that magic had no place in New Scots, but though she tried to deny it, magic is in her blood and bone. Orphaned and alone, she uses her forbidden magic to summon the spirit of her father. He sends her to find a friend from his past and a new place in the world, but to complete the journey, she will need help that comes in the form of a surly and mysterious stranger.

To Erika and Nat, my friends and sisters.
— Sarah

CHAPTER ONE

Claire stopped her long walk and sank to her knees in the snow. The wet coldness seeped into her stockings, but she was so distracted she hardly noticed. She had to be far enough away now.

She dug her trembling fingers into her pocket and pulled out some matches and a candle. *The* candle. Claire took a deep breath and held it as she lit a match and moved it to the wick.

She had heard about this ritual, and desperately wanted it to work. The man she had secretly bought the candle from assured her it would—*if* she had magic inside her.

The magic was the big unknown. She had never tried to use it or access it at all since she had sworn off it long ago. Everyone knew magic users met terrible ends. Claire knew that from personal experience, both old and new. She had always believed there was nothing worth that risk. Until now.

The candle caught, the slightly acrid scent of smoke

drifting toward her. She closed her eyes and spoke the words. With a last desperate hope, she opened her eyes and looked up, heart tugging between pain and relief. His spirit was in front of her, smile just as she remembered. She whispered softly as her eyes began to blur, "Hello, Father."

"Claire Bear."

Her breath hitched. Instead of the deep soothing timbre she had always heard from him in life, his voice was now whisper-thin. But the tone and words were the same, and it began to crack open the rift grief had caused inside her.

She took a deep breath and forced the tears back, then tried to speak normally. Her candle would only last so long, and she had so much she needed to say and hear in return.

"Father, do you know about Mother and..." She closed her eyes and swallowed before whispering, "and James?"

"Yes."

Claire shook herself as she opened her eyes. Time, she told herself firmly, was not on her side. Not today.

"You know what happened?"

The translucent form shifted closer to her. Dare she hope it was to comfort her? She really didn't know much about how this ritual worked.

"Yes."

"All Mother told me before she died was that I needed to talk to you—that there was something important I needed to do, and only you could tell me. She made me swear to do this ritual so I could ask."

She heaved a breath before standing up, wincing now at the cold encompassing her body. Her clothing wasn't nearly warm enough to be rolling in the snow, but she hadn't been thinking clearly earlier.

Claire looked at the spirit of her father, all that remained of him, and fiercely wished that life was just and fair so that her family could still be with her. But while on occasion life was just, fairness rarely existed, and definitely not in New Scots.

"So, Father, what am I to do?"

He looked at her, and she could have sworn his ghostly eyes were full of pride and pain. The pain she could understand, and she hoped the pride might be for her. It had been several long months since her father had died, and every day she longed for him to come back. There was no bringing back the dead, though. Even a spirit was on borrowed time.

"There was so much I should have told you. So much you needed to learn." His fingers touched her cheek, and she felt a gentle whisper of movement and a coolness that numbed her already cold face before he lowered his hand.

She swallowed, but stayed silent. Regrets were an indulgence at the moment. She glanced down at the candle and saw it was already two-thirds gone. Too little time left. She looked back and saw that her father had noticed the candle as well when he nodded.

"I had an old…friend you need to find, who can tell you more of what you need to know. He gave her directions to reach "John the Saint."

Claire squinted in confusion. "Your friend is a priest named John?"

He tilted his head the way he used to when she said

something silly, but it looked very odd on a spirit. "No, his name is Andrew."

She shook her head, reminding herself she couldn't waste time. "I don't know if I can get there by myself. I've never left New Scots, and have barely been out of Hafox. This trip will take days. Are you sure I need to go see this guy?"

If a spirit could look alarmed, her father did now. "You *must*, Claire. It's the most important thing you will ever do. I already made arrangements for you in case something happened to me."

"All right, what arrangements?"

He seemed relieved that she had agreed so quickly, but didn't heave a breath as others would in their relief. It gave Claire an odd feeling and reminded her again that her father wasn't really here, only his spirit.

"You will find your guide in town. His name is Logan Markham."

Claire groaned. "Daaad!" she whined. "Why did you choose *him*? He's so creepy! He just wanders around town and watches people."

"*Claire Drucilla Montgomery*! What did your mother and I teach you about being judgmental?" His form looked stronger, his expression making it alarmingly clear that he was angry.

She blew out a breath and mumbled, just as she had when he'd scolded her in life. "That it's an exercise of small-mindedness and lacks compassion."

He nodded. "Just meet with him and suspend judgment until you've reached Andrew. Then if you still think he's creepy, it will be based on fact, not prejudice, gossip, or conjecture."

She gave him a small smile. "Fair enough, Father."

He moved forward until she felt his ghostly energy around her, apparently trying to hug her. Rather than chilling her, she received a surprising boost of warmth. She put the arm that didn't hold the candle where she thought he might be to hug him back. It wasn't the same, but it was something.

When he pulled back, his form was as faint as it had been when he'd first appeared. "Father, Dad, Papa. Call me whatever you like, but know I love you forever, Claire Be—."

He disappeared just after the candle went out, leaving her staring into the dark, empty forest in front of her and holding a useless nub of wax.

"I love you too, Papa."

CHAPTER TWO

After a quick stop at home to pack, Claire went to meet her guide. Halfway to her destination, Claire paused and wondered what she was doing. She had lost her family and likely lost her home. She had performed a ritual that confirmed she had magic—magic that she had long hated and now apparently needed to come to terms with. She'd been told she needed to travel to some stranger who would tell her about this mysterious task she needed to do, guided by another stranger she had always heard odd tales of.

If anyone had told her this months ago, she would have called them crazy and tried to forget it. No one would want such a life, or at least no one in New Scots. Everyone here tried to be as normal as possible, so there was no disruption.

The truth was, they all lived in fear that they might be accused of having magic. Once suggested, the suspicion was inflamed, fueled by gossip till it could no longer be ignored. In that case, the subject was usually brutally killed by vigilantes in the community.

She hated it.

Claire stopped walking when she realized her tears had blurred her vision. Her mother had always been wise and kind, even to those who didn't seem to deserve it. She didn't understand how anyone could—

She pushed those memories away again and struggled to get herself back under control. She needed to leave, and this wasn't helping. Still. Her mother had been right about how to respond to others' fear. Hate wouldn't do anything except make her bitter.

She meandered purposefully through the streets, hoping to keep from attracting attention, as well as to lose anyone if they happened to follow her. Finally, she reached her intended destination— the house of Logan Markham, the man her father had told her could guide her on this journey.

Avoiding the front of the house since it was in plain view, she went to the rear and finally came to the back door, which was shaded by a large tree. The sky was in the final stages of sunrise before turning all to blue. The gorgeous colors distracted her from knocking.

Finally, she shook herself and lifted her hand—just as the door opened to a shadowed figure framed in the doorway.

"You're late. I expected you hours ago."

CHAPTER THREE

"Excuse me?" Claire gasped. "How did you even know to expect me?"

The man who had to be Logan Markham withdrew into the house. "Come on in, sweetheart. We have things to do and places to be."

She stepped into the room, able to see the man a little better now that there was more light from the windows across the room as well as from the door behind her. She stopped next to him and looked up six inches to glare into his face.

"How did you know I was coming?" She narrowed her eyes. "And don't call me sweetheart."

The man grinned, looking younger than she had expected. The times she had seen him in the past he had a full beard, but now he was clean shaven, which took ten years off his apparent age. His blue eyes glinted in the morning sun, and his brown hair was a bit disorderly. He likely cut it himself. On any other morning, she would have been amused. As it was, she merely raised her eyebrows as she waited.

"Your father gave me instructions, of course."

"Then you *are* Logan Markham."

He raised an eyebrow of his own as he shut the door and crossed his arms. "Don't be stupid."

"From sweetheart to stupid. That was fast."

His mouth quirked. "Well, you said not to call you sweetheart." He sobered completely. "I talked to your father several months before he died, when he expressed concern about your situation. I almost expected a visit from you all after your father died, but I didn't hear from any of you. When the events of yesterday came to my attention, I figured I should be prepared."

He grabbed her pack from her shoulder and hefted it, ignoring her startled squawk of outrage. Claire stood there fuming while he quickly placed a few more items into it, attached what appeared to be a bedroll, and handed it back to her. "Try that on and see if it's too heavy."

She glared at him a moment more, but he merely raised an eyebrow with an air of patience that could last all day. Muttering words her mother would likely box her ears for, she grabbed the pack and shrugged it over her shoulders as he occupied himself with putting a few more things in his own pack and fastening it shut.

Throwing the pack over the shoulder of his long brown overcoat, he looked around the house one more time and nodded. Gesturing for her to follow, he exited the house and shut the door after her. He did something to the door while he murmured words too low for her to hear. By the time he finished and turned to go, the hair on her arms felt as if it were standing at attention.

She grabbed his arm as he walked past her—subconsciously noticing that his arm felt more muscular than it appeared—and narrowed her eyes. "What was that?"

He looked down at her for a long moment, his face completely unreadable, then moved forward, easily pulling his arm out of her grip. "What was what?"

She followed him out of the yard as she struggled with words to explain, then finally threw her hands up. "I don't know! *That.*"

"*That* is not something I'm going to discuss right now." He looked around, and she noticed there were people walking on the roads now that the sun was high enough in the sky. "Certainly not here."

If it were something magic related, which was highly likely considering her body's reaction, she could completely understand his reticence. "Fair enough," she finally responded. "But we *are* going to talk about it." She spoke firmly so he understood she wasn't going to just let it go.

Disappointingly, the glance he threw her looked more amused than quelled. She sped up so she could walk next to him rather than following him like a child, and they walked in silence for several long minutes as they headed toward the northwest side of town. Drifts of snow lay piled next to the buildings, though the streets were mostly passable. The people they walked by gave them a critical eye when they noticed the packs the two wore, but they were left alone.

"So, why did my father ask *you?*"

The look he gave her showed irritation mixed with disdain. She reviewed the words in her head and realized the way she had said them might have indicated there was something wrong or lacking in him. She reddened in embarrassment and shame.

"I'm sorry, that didn't come out how I meant it. I just never heard my father talk about you before he died and wondered why he had asked you to help us."

He was quiet for several long moments, causing Claire to wonder if he was angry, before he responded, "He *didn't* ask. I offered."

Claire stopped walking, her mouth hanging open as she stared at him in astonishment. "What? Why?"

He moved a few more steps down the road before he stopped, his face unreadable stone and his jaw set. "I had my reasons."

She walked a few steps toward him. "And those would be?"

His eyes changed color slightly as he stared at her, his face taking on more of a fierce wildness. "Mine." His mouth formed almost a snarl around the word as he leaned forward, causing her eyes to widen in surprise.

She lifted her hands—to stop him or calm him, she didn't know—and spoke softly. "All right, I get it. Your reasons were your own. I'm not going to ask again."

The wildness left him as he watched her, and she saw surprise in his face. "Thank you."

"Sure."

As the word left her mouth, a scuffing sound behind them startled them both, causing them to whirl toward it. Two men approached them from an alley nearby, one man carrying a pipe he held in both hands and the other holding a knife.

Glancing around, she saw no one else on the street. They had all scurried away at the first sign of trouble.

Leaving them alone.

CHAPTER FOUR

"Give us the packs there, kids, an' ya won' be hurt."

The men coming toward them were older and had scars and tattoos, their clothing and teeth showing they had no acquaintance whatsoever with basic hygiene.

Claire swallowed, then swung her head the other direction when she heard movement there, revealing another man who held a badly-made sword. He was uglier, bigger, and stronger than the first two, though not any better acquainted with soap and water. She groaned, realizing they had stopped to have a disagreement in the one place her father had told her never to come, let alone linger.

"Why did we come this direction?" She swiveled her head between their assailants as the three men came closer.

"This is the way to our destination." Claire was surprised to hear Logan sounding calm, and glanced back to see him holding out a staff that was perfect for her height.

Her eyes widened. "Where did this come from?"

He put it in her hands. "Take it. See if you can fend the first two off while I take care of the other one." He nodded at the two men and turned back to the bigger man, pulling a knife she hadn't noticed out of his belt.

"What am I supposed to do with this?" she yelled at his back.

He turned his head slightly, enough to throw his voice back. "Figure it out, sweetheart."

She muttered curses at him that he couldn't have heard, although he laughed for the first time in her hearing, so he must have picked up something.

"And don't call me sweetheart!" she growled.

Logan chuckled as she turned back to the two men. They were within a few feet of her now, eying her and each other as if not sure who should go first or do what.

"Have you made up your minds, gentleman?" She leaned on the staff just a touch as she looked at the two men. The man on her left had greasy black hair and a beard. The man on her right looked at her with a gleam she didn't like at all, although he was slightly better groomed than the bearded fellow. She heard fighting behind her.

"Oh, yes." The lusty man grinned. "We're definitely taking it all." The other man grinned back and giggled as he hefted his pipe.

Claire shrugged. "Ok, then. Just making sure."

Without any warning, she kicked up the bottom of her staff, twisted, and jammed it into lusty man's stomach, then whipped it up toward his face as he bent over with a groan. The edge caught his chin, whipping his head back, and she twirled the staff in her hands and hit the man over the head. He fell like a rock.

The man with the pipe gaped as she brought the staff over to meet his nose, eliciting a shriek as he fell to his knees. He dropped the pipe to hold his hands over his face. Another twist of the staff and he joined his compatriot on the ground. She stepped to the other side of their bodies and nudged the two, but they were out cold.

Claire turned then leaned lightly on her staff again. The two large men were standing side by side, having paused their fight to watch her. The big ugly brute stared at her slender form in astonishment, while Logan Markham eyed her with a gleam not unlike that of the lusty thug on the ground in front of her. Strangely, she didn't mind quite so much.

"Need any help?" She smiled sweetly.

His face turned to stone again. He took a half step and pulled the man's sword arm across his body with his left hand while he backhanded the man's face with his right, which still held the knife. The man cried out and dropped to the ground after getting the pommel to the head.

Logan smirked as he walked toward her, sheathing his knife. "Nope."

"Ok, then." She twirled the staff in her hands as she watched him. "Thanks for the staff. It was rather useful."

"Happy to help." He paused a few steps in front of her and gestured to the side, indicating she should continue on. She stepped forward, kicking the lusty man in the head with her boot again when he moaned. The sound subsided immediately.

She received a raised eyebrow from Logan.

"Just making sure my displeasure with being 'taken' is made known."

His face turned thunderous as he took a step forward, but she hooked his elbow and pulled him with her down the street. "I took care of it already. Let's get out of here."

He muttered darkly under his breath but walked with her as they moved on, pulling his arm away.

Sometime later she took the easterly road that led to New Brawn. Hearing a cough behind her, she turned back to see Logan gesturing in the other direction. "This way."

She frowned, wondering what he was playing at. "This is the way my father told me to go."

Logan nodded, his hair bouncing with the movement and the slight wind. "And it will get you there." He gestured behind him. "This way will cut almost two days off our journey."

Claire hesitated. If she continued on, she would be following her father's directions. If she followed Logan, she would be entirely dependent on his guidance. What did she know about the man, anyway?

"Are you sure you aren't taking me somewhere just to have your way with me?"

His face looked more wild at the reminder of the thug they'd left behind, but then cleared and he gave her a lazy grin. "Sweetheart, if that was my intention, we wouldn't have had to go anywhere. I had a perfectly comfortable bed back at my house."

She pursed her lips in thought before walking toward him—to follow the road he indicated. "True."

As she pulled even with the man, who had begun walking next to her, she stretched her staff out to sweep his knees just enough for his legs to buckle. He staggered a few steps.

"Don't call me sweetheart," she threw over her shoulder as she continued walking.

The muttered cursing behind her made her smile.

CHAPTER FIVE

Claire looked out from the rock she sat on with her knees drawn up in front of her. They were camped at the tip of a peninsula that jutted into the middle of the bay, and she watched the deep pinks, blues, and purples of the sunset behind the clouds.

She heard slight noises to indicate that Logan was moving around the fire behind her. The two of them had traveled for hours before reaching a tiny abandoned harbor where he had a small rowboat hidden in some brush. They had reached their current campsite just as the sun hit the trees in the distance, completely distracting Claire for the better part of an hour.

"Ready for some food?"

His voice startled her since a peaceful quiet had crept up on her while she watched the sunset. Turning her head, she saw Logan holding out a steaming mug with a utensil standing up in it. Claire's stomach let out a moaning growl of protest. She straightened in surprise, pressing a hand to her belly.

"Apparently so." She accepted the offered mug and sniffed at the stew. "Thank you." She scooted over in case he decided to join her on the large rock. There weren't many other seating options. She adjusted her position, so the edges of the rock weren't digging into her skin.

Logan stood for a moment but finally sat down stiffly on the other end of the rock. He turned slightly away, so she mostly saw his back and the side of his face. After a few blows to cool the stew, she took a bite and found it surprisingly tasty, making a noise of appreciation that drew a tiny smile from the man.

"Did your father teach you how to fight?"

"Oh, we're talking now, are we?" Claire couldn't help teasing him since she had tried for almost an hour to get the man to say something—anything—as they walked earlier in the day. He had completely closed down for some reason she had yet to ascertain. Still, if she answered some questions, perhaps he would give her information in return. This man was a huge question mark she was surprised to find herself curious about.

Logan responded now with a faint smile she could barely see in the last light of the day. Hopefully, he recognized how ridiculous it had been and wouldn't give her his stone-face impression again. She would be happy to see that look go.

"Yes, some of it. My mother also taught us, to the surprise of anyone who knew her."

"I never met your mother," he responded slowly as if he

were trying to be careful with his words. "Why was it so surprising that she taught you how to fight?"

Claire coughed a laugh, thinking how ironic it was to have a graceful and kind woman with little to no attitude ruthlessly teach her daughter throws and holds designed to fell men twice her size. She tried to explain this to Logan and found herself rambling on sometime later about a time her brother James refused to fight his mother, their emptied mugs sitting beside them.

"And my mother just looked at James—this woman about my height, but gentle and wise, looked up at her six-foot-tall, strong son—and he just wilted." She chuckled and was warmed to hear Logan laughing with her. "He never refused to fight after that."

"Did he ever win?" His voice sounded intense.

"Oh, no. Mother always won. Or I did."

That elicited a grunt.

Claire tilted her head and peered at him even though she could barely make the man out in the firelight. "Why so interested?"

She felt more than saw his shrug. "Just curious. It's not every day a girl fells two men in less than fifteen seconds."

Claire stared at Logan for a moment, letting him know she wasn't buying it, but couldn't resist. "It sure seemed to distract *you*. That man could have popped you in the head while you weren't looking."

Logan twisted his body around to face her, his strength evident in the quick move. "I was paying attention."

She smiled in amusement at his defensive tone. "Sure you were."

He frowned. "I *was*."

"I agreed with you." Claire grinned. Teasing him was even more fun than teasing James. That thought deflated her as the grief rose, amusement disappearing entirely.

Logan picked up on her mood shift. "I'm sorry." He held himself a little stiffly, but she sensed he was trying to comfort her.

"It wasn't your fault." If anything, his body became more rigid, not less. She shrugged, not knowing what else to say.

They sat there for another moment before she began to feel uncomfortable, both from her position on the rock and the measure of silence between them.

"Well, I'm going to try to sleep." She slid to the ground and began to walk over to her pack. When he didn't move, she turned back. "Goodnight."

His form remained so still and stiff he could have been cut from the rock he sat on. Huffing a breath, she spread her bedroll before the fire, muttering comments about stoic men and their silences. It took a moment to realize that the snow had been cleared from around the fire and a few bows of evergreen had been laid on either side so they wouldn't lay on the cold ground.

Well, now she felt bad for thinking negative thoughts about the man.

Rolling herself up, she turned to face the fire, becoming mesmerized by the flickers of flame. As she began to drop off to sleep, she had a final thought.

Logan definitely had secrets.

She hoped none of them would bite her.

CHAPTER SIX

Claire slept the sleep of the physically and emotionally exhausted, knowing nothing at all until Logan woke her the next morning. He was still as silent as he had been the night before, which put her in a wonderfully irritable mood. If he wasn't going to talk, she wasn't going to make him. Light-and-snarky Logan was a lot easier to handle than dark-and-broody Logan.

After rowing across the rest of the bay, they spoke little as they took a snow laden path to the southwest that only he could see, apparently. She could barely tell there was a track as they walked. The undergrowth that had built up over the last decades certainly helped to disguise it, but the snow had topped it off. Finally, hours after lunch, she saw shimmers of light in the distance.

When they emerged from the forest, there was a town that had been largely left to decay on a harbor at the edge of a bay. Claire followed Logan toward it, becoming so distracted by the glimpses of lives from the distant past that she eventually ended up running to catch up. She couldn't get over how much had been left to rot.

Her father had told her stories of the World's Worst Day Ever, the day the world had stopped. Nothing had ever been the same after that. What was even worse was that just when humanity had started to recover, they had entered the mad times. Her mother had shuddered every time someone had hinted about those. Claire lived in a time that wasn't great, but from the few stories she had heard and the history taught in school, she was lucky to have missed that time altogether.

Logan didn't stop to wait for her. Perhaps he didn't want to linger in this eerie graveyard of houses, or perhaps he couldn't wait to be done with the task that he had volunteered for. The thought sank into her stomach like a small weight, but she didn't know what to do with it. She did what she had always done when faced with uncertainty —shoved it to the side and kept walking.

James had called it being stubbornly stupid.

James.

Her steps faltered for a moment.

Claire shoved those thoughts to the side too.

It wasn't until the travelers reached the outskirts of the town that Claire began to see movement. A few streets later there was a lot more activity, people ambling from one place to another. Strangely, many of the inhabitants were well over the age of thirty, and most were over forty. There were no children or young people in view, and the noise level was strangely low for the number of people visible.

Logan led them on a side street that bypassed the

middle of town. Claire couldn't help feeling guilty at her relief in passing fewer people, but it was rather creepy to see these inhabitants and hear little sound to note their passage. She couldn't believe how much of a difference in atmosphere she saw between this town and her own city of Hafox.

After a few more turns, they reached a street with a few shops along the sides. Logan veered off the road when he saw the grocery store and glided across the empty lot in front. Her father had told her these empty spaces were for ancient machines to gather while waiting for their owners. It had always sounded like a fantasy tale to Claire.

An older woman looked up in surprise as the two crossed the threshold, ringing a bell that had seen far better days. She glanced between them several times in awe and amazement...and more than a hint of fear, causing Claire to grow uneasy. She stood back and waited while Logan stepped forward to greet the woman.

"I was told you could direct us to Andrew Cormack?"

The woman blinked, the many lines on her face drawing in. "Andrew Cormack?" She looked puzzled as she repeated the name several times with her withered lips. Finally, her eyes cleared. "Ah! Old Andy!" She nodded eagerly.

As she gave Logan the directions, Claire couldn't help noticing odd mannerisms about the woman in front of them. She came across both old and young, her mannerisms those of a younger person while her movements were those of an older person.

Even though they hadn't bought anything, the lady thanked the two weary travelers for coming in several times, her fingers fluttering nervously in the air. Claire was just relieved to leave the shop as they stepped back out. She rolled her shoulders a few times to release the tension and sighed as she jogged to catch up with Logan, who hadn't stopped moving.

"Hold up."

The increasingly infuriating man slowed slightly but continued down the street, following the directions the woman gave. Claire glanced at him once she caught up. Logan's face was concerned, and his eyebrows were drawn.

"You thought that was weird and creepy too, right?"

He tilted his head to look at her, blue eyes steady but concerned. "There was something off, yes."

Claire shared her observation that the woman seemed both old and young at the same time. Logan's face cleared. "Yes, that was what I sensed. She was also nervous and afraid, but she didn't lie."

"I saw that too, but it didn't make sense. You aren't *that* scary."

She saw a flicker of amusement on his face as they turned onto another street. "I'm not scary?"

"Ehh." Claire shrugged and brought her fingers together to indicate a small amount. She was pleased to see more of a smile on his face, even if it was still tiny.

"I can be scary." He spoke so matter of fact she wondered how often people actually talked to him about the subject. Probably not that often.

"Oh, sure, you can beat a guy. You took care of that thug easily enough. But scary?" She scoffed.

He stopped suddenly, causing her to halt her own fast walk. He looked more intense than amused now. He took a step forward, almost but not quite into her personal space, and his eyes flashed and bore into her.

"I have tried to maintain a level of civility over the last years, but make no mistake, Claire." He bit out the words, and he seemed wilder. "I can be as scary as any bastard you've ever come across."

The intensity and growl in his voice as he pushed his face closer to hers made her believe him. Part of her was scared at what she saw in his eyes and wanted to shake. Another part of her rose up and wouldn't allow her to do anything but stand there in front of him and fake a yawn.

"All right, you're a scary bastard. Are we close yet?"

He sniffed all of a sudden and peered at her in slight confusion, then he snorted and turned down a shaded street with only a few houses.

"You have no sense of self-preservation."

She remained silent this time as she followed him.

She wasn't entirely sure he was wrong.

CHAPTER SEVEN

A few minutes later Claire followed Logan up the lawn of a small home that seemed typical for this town, patched with any spare material from times past that could be found. The result was an interesting if eclectic mix of style.

They stood on the small porch waiting for an answer to their knock, alternately eying each other and glancing away. Logan stood rather stiffly, as if he regretted the point he had made moments ago. Claire shifted back and forth on her feet.

Claire heard a soft, "I'm sorry." Her glance flew up to meet his melancholy blue eyes. She didn't have a chance to ask what he was sorry for before the door opened beside them.

They turned to face the figure standing in the doorway. He was short for a man, only an inch or so above her own height, but he had a presence that made him seem taller. His untidy gray hair flopped down, obscuring his eyes for a moment. The voice that sounded through his gray beard was gruff, but kindly all the same. His posture indicated that he was used to standing straight and tall, though his age now made that difficult. He looked like a faded version of his younger self.

"What are you young people doing here?"

Claire's mouth worked, but she couldn't speak. Thankfully, Logan came to her rescue.

"Claire has come to see you."

"Claire?" His once-strong hand impatiently moved his hair out of his eyes, revealing dark-gray irises that looked familiar.

They were her father's eyes.

The eyes she had inherited widened as she gasped. The older man looked at her with both happiness and alarm.

"Who are you?" she whispered, almost afraid to ask.

His hands trembled as he started to reach out to her, then jerked them back. He blinked to stifle the tears that began to flood his eyes. Stepping back, he motioned for them to come in.

When Claire entered, she got the sense of time standing still. The whole room was a mismatched collection of furniture and belongings. It was a relatively small house with the living room, kitchen, and eating area all in one large room, and what Claire supposed were a bedroom and bathroom off to the side. A fireplace graced the living area. She placed her staff by the door and took her backpack off, setting it by the wall. Logan followed suit.

"Please, have a seat."

There were few options, only a cushioned chair that was obviously used often and a short bench. Toward the back was a chair by the small eating table. Claire took the short bench, leaving the cushioned chair for the man they had come to see. Logan hesitated for a moment, then brought the chair from the table over to sit between the two.

Claire quietly stared at the elderly man as he lowered himself into the cushioned chair. He cleared his throat, looking nervous as he tugged first on his tattered sweater, then on his faded and worn pants. Finally, he looked up at Claire and flinched as his eyes connected with hers.

"You look so much like your father," he began tentatively, as if he wasn't sure how she would react. "I had almost forgotten."

"How do you know my father?"

The older man opened his mouth a few times before shrugging.

"I'm his brother."

Claire's mouth dropped open. "You're my uncle?" Beside them, she felt Logan becoming more alert and focusing intently on the older man, whose mouth moved self-deprecatingly.

"Yes."

"But you're…"

"Old?" He raised his gray eyebrows in amusement.

She flushed. "Well, yes. Older than my father looked, anyway."

He sighed. "That's a long story."

She crossed her arms pointedly. "I have nowhere else to be."

He took a breath, sadness growing on his face. "I'm assuming your father is dead. He wouldn't have sent you here otherwise."

Claire flinched at his words as she struggled with her emotions. "Yes. All of them are."

He looked startled. "All of them?"

She jerked a nod, and her body stiffened. "Father, Mother, and my...brother James."

Her uncle's face crumbled. "I'm sorry to hear that, Claire."

"Mother taught me how to use a spirit candle to see Father. He told me to come to you."

The man snorted. "Spirit candles aren't real, girl. That magic was all you."

"What?" Her eyes went wide, but she shook her head. "Please just tell me what's going on. Why did you never come to visit us even though you aren't that far away? Why did my father tell me to come here after he died? What is this task he talked about that only I can do? Does it have to do with that magic? And why is this town so creepy?" Her voice rose with each question until she was almost shouting at the end.

Her uncle stilled, then swallowed before answering. "All right. It has everything to do with your magic. It's all the same story. Just...understand that this is difficult for me." He eyed her appraisingly. "I think it might be difficult for you too."

"Please."

His shoulders slumped, then he took a breath to begin.

"Your father and I were brothers." He paused for a moment. "Your father was the oldest, then our brother Wyatt, Grace, me, and...Julian."

He swallowed and asked Logan, "Would you mind

getting me some water, boy, and for you both if you'd like?" He gestured to the kitchen.

Logan nodded, then rose to move toward the kitchen while Andrew—Andy?—continued.

Claire raised a hand before he could begin speaking. "I'm sorry, Uncle." His eyes lit up for a moment, then faded at her next words. "I can't help noticing you are speaking of them in the past tense."

His eyes looked grief-stricken and regretful. "That's because they are all dead except one. And he's dead to me."

Her eyes widened in surprise. "What happened?"

Her uncle hesitated, his hands trembling. It took a moment for her to realize it was anger.

"Julian killed them with his magic."

CHAPTER EIGHT

Claire gasped. "He killed *all* of them?"

Andrew closed his eyes as he collapsed back into the chair and nodded. "Mother and Father too."

Logan walked back with three chipped and repaired cups that looked salvaged. He distributed them, and they drank for a time.

Andrew placed his cup on the small table next to him. There was nowhere for Logan and Claire to put their cups, so they held onto them as the story continued.

"Did your father ever tell you of the time when the magic began?"

Claire thought for a moment, then shook her head. "Only vague mentions."

"Your father was born around the time the magic began. We children were born a year apart." He snorted. "Mother had her hands full with us. By the time Julian came into the world, the magic was at its full strength."

He took another swallow of water. "We never knew

why. Maybe it was just the way the magic worked, but our town had a surplus of children around the same time. Beginning with your father and ending with Julian, dozens of babies were born to the residents. Our parents struggled to provide enough food for everyone, so we had difficult years for a while. It wasn't until the older children reached the age of five that the adults began to notice that these children were…different." He paused.

Claire thought her uncle looked haunted by what happened all those years ago.

"How were they different, Uncle?"

He blinked and turned his head to meet her eyes. "They saw spirits."

"What?" She straightened, moving her arm forward before remembering she still held the cup. She took a gulp of water and cleared her throat. Talk of magic had always made her nervous. "How could they do that?"

The old man spread his gnarled and wrinkled hands. "Magic."

Claire tightened her hand on the cup. "I don't understand."

The old man leaned forward, gray eyes like her own staring at her. "I told you earlier that spirit candles aren't real. Ever since our town showed everyone it was possible to see spirits, those looking to make money have sold them. It's the magic inside you that makes them work.

"All of the children born at that time developed the ability to talk to spirits, and a few of the adults too. It's where the rumors of being able to talk to spirits came from." He spread his hands. "We did nothing to gain that magic except be born."

Logan finally spoke up. "Where did it go wrong?"

Andrew sank in on himself and brought his hands up to cover his face. Claire couldn't help but feel sorry for what the man was reliving, but she had to know. She waited, hoping he would continue on his own.

Finally, he lowered his hands, revealing a tear-marked face. "Some of the children couldn't handle this ability. They went insane before they were even ten years old, unable to tell what was real and what wasn't. They became stuck in their minds and grew almost catatonic, not responding to anyone. More than a third of the children were affected this way."

Claire felt horrified, and she shuddered. Logan began watching her out of the corner of his eye, face stoic and blank except for a tightening in his jaw.

Her uncle continued, lost in his memories and oblivious to her reaction. "Some of the children handled the change well and were able to use their new abilities to contact those who had been lost. They were the lucky ones, at least at first," he whispered.

She straightened, not liking the look in his eyes. "What do you mean?"

"A few of the children were strong in this new magic, with Julian being the strongest—possibly because he was the last born, at the height of the dawn of magic." He shook his head slowly. "Even now I still don't know what caused him to make the choices he did. As Julian grew in power and understanding of his magic, he also grew in cruelty, becoming utterly dismissive of anyone else's opinion or their right to choose for themselves."

Claire began to ask a question, but his next grief-stricken words stopped her cold. "He was only five years old the first time he killed."

Claire and Logan both straightened in their seats. "Who was it?" Claire whispered.

"Grace." He took a big breath and let it out. "We didn't realize it until later. Much later. It devastated our family. Mother and Father withdrew into themselves after she died, which wasn't good in the long run. Maybe he could have been stopped if they had paid more attention.

"Every so often a child would die, throwing everyone into confusion and depression. One by one, the adults all grew prematurely old. It wasn't until your father was fifteen that we realized their state wasn't a result of mere grief, but something crueler and more sinister."

Andrew met her eyes. "Several years later, your father figured out what was happening and put together the pieces that led to Julian. By then, it was too late to reverse the damage and many people in the town were dead."

She blinked, trying to understand. "But what was he doing? How did he kill them all without anyone knowing?"

He just looked at her, and she sensed he was reluctant to tell her for some reason. Logan had been still and quiet the whole time. She glanced at her traveling companion, curious as to his thoughts, to find him watching her. She felt she could almost see the thoughts moving through his head one after another, although they were so quick she was certain he was purposely squelching them.

Oh, yes. She no longer thought him creepy, but Logan Markham definitely had secrets. Secrets she wanted to know.

Her head went back toward her uncle as he began to speak, breaking the connection between her and Logan.

"He was using the magic all of us had been given."

Claire tried to focus her thoughts, but it was difficult. She shook her head to clear it. "The spirit magic? How could that be used to kill someone? It's only used to see dead people."

She was shaken to the core.

"Everyone has a spirit, especially those who are still alive."

EPILOGUE

Claire stood outside the house later, arms wrapped around herself, staring at the quiet town and listening to the silence. So *that* was why there were hardly any people in the town, and why they all looked so much older. This strange magic, the magic her father and his siblings had acquired, had been used to steal their spirits. Their life and energy.

The same magic that flowed through her.

She felt more than heard someone move closer to her over the snow. From the pace, she expected her newfound uncle.

"Is that my task, then? To stop Julian from using his evil magic to kill everyone?"

Suppressing a shudder, she turned to see Andrew's eyes droop in weariness and fear, but he shook his head.

"It's what you do with the magic that makes it good or evil. But no, my child. I fear your task is much greater than that, though dealing with Julian will be a large part of your near-future."

His eyes met hers and she froze, chills sweeping her that had nothing to do with the cold weather. Her uncle was afraid *for* her, but he was also afraid *of* her.

"I'm sorry. I'm so very sorry, but nothing will ever be the same for you again."

AUTHOR NOTES S.E. WEIR

I had this idea for a short story in the Age of Magic shortly after the last *Fans Write* Volume came out. I clipped along writing it, and around the time Claire knocked on Logan's door, I realized this story had more to tell than a short.

I kept writing; I just couldn't stop. It unfolded before my eyes, and every word I wrote pulled idea after idea as to what Claire's world would be like in the Age of Magic. I have story ideas and character arcs for at least three and a half books; this story you read is just the start. I eventually had to set the story aside as another one was being called out, which I hope you will have in your hands very soon.

At midnight on submission day, I decided to simplify what I had written so far and show the steps that led Claire to discover what the future holds. I hope you enjoyed reading it! I would love to write the rest of the story and find out Claire's destiny and what secrets Logan is hiding. Maybe at some point!

Thank you to all the fans who have also written stories for our FansWrite projects, which you may have already read. You all are so inspiring. Keep writing and chasing your dreams!

Thank you, Chris and Lee, for helping to create an awesome world in which to dream and write. I really appreciate how encouraging and helpful you both are.

Thank you, thank you to Erika Everest and Nat Roberts, my partners in crime...ahem, I mean in writing, of course! And being admins for FansWrite, and everything else our minds dream up each week. I can't imagine doing this without you.

Thank you so very much to Steve Campbell and Lynne Stiegler. You two are the glue that holds us together and the wind that helps us fly! Without you both, we would be in a sad state.

Many, many thanks to Michael Anderle, the boss man, and the source of inspiration for all of the stories we have all submitted. No matter how busy you are, you make time to respond, always with a kind word—and often one that makes me laugh. Thank you!

No thanks are complete without mentioning my other half, the best man I know. He doesn't always understand my drive to write and how I can sit dreaming up stories for so long, but I know he is proud of me, and he will often ask if I need time to write. (For future reference, the answer is always yes. ;)) Love and thanks to you, my husband!

And thanks to you, the reader. I can hear the jokes in my head. If a story is told, but no one hears or reads it... You all are just as inspiring as everyone already mentioned.

I hope you enjoyed reading *Spirit Whisperer* as much as I enjoyed writing it!

Sarah

ADMIN NOTES – THE SISTERS THREE

It's been just over a year since Fans Write KGU first began! Can you believe we are now on Volume 3 with a volume for the Oriceran Universe underway? As of this publication we will have published twenty-five short stories with two poems and *lots* of haikus. Craziness! Crazy Awesomeness to be exact.

Nothing this big comes together without effort. We would like to thank Michael for trusting us with this project and giving us the scope to grow it. Steve Campbell is the unsung hero behind the scenes keeping the logistical wheels turning, and the JIT team consistently help us make all the stories better. (Though if there is anything we missed, please let us know by contacting Readers-Help@kurtherianbooks.com.) Jeff Brown once again went to work on the cover design initially created by himself and Andrew Dobell to bring a fresh look for volume 3 while maintaining the consistency with previous volumes – and we love the purple! Finally, a very special thanks to

Lynne Stiegler – editor extraordinaire, custodian of canon (and boy, those were some lively discussions!), a great friend and also the author of the many haikus scattered throughout this volume! Thank you all for your support and input, you guys rock!

Right now we, the Admins and co., are working on the Oriceran volume coming out in December. Stories are already being posted there, which makes us happy, happy! Shortly after this publication, we will begin our mad dash for the submission deadline in October. If you are interested in joining us, see the link down below. It's a whole different universe compared to KGU, so there are different rules, but the stories will be no less fun and exciting! We, the fans want that for the writers, ourselves, and you, the readers. Please join in! We're all a little mad there, but it's the best kind – promise!

In November, we the Admins, aka the Sisters Three, will be attending the 20Booksto50k conference in Vegas. What's the best part? You are all cordially invited to attend the Fans Meet and Greet the Authors event on Thursday, November 8, 2018 from 3-5pm at Sam's Town Hotel & Gambling Hall! We are having our own Fans Write party there, as authors from across all three volumes will be there, many of us meeting each other for the first time! As well as the Sisters Three, other Fans Write attendees include Tim Bischoff, Tracey Byrnes, Logan Caird, Micky Cocker, James Gartside, Samantha Harmer, and Dominic Novielli, and of course Michael, Craig and many of our other LMBPN authors (and many others) will be there too and we would love to meet you all! Wahooo!!

Michael and the Sisters Three also have a huge

announcement that we will make during the conference and again at the meet and greet! It will be our own party within a party as we celebrate exciting things to come! You don't want to miss it!

What comes after the conference and next year? We have nothing nailed down enough to tell you yet, but there is one thing we can say. We've got plans, my pretties! Ideas we've kicked around, things more set in stone than not, but you can definitely count on there being more KGU anthologies! We aren't done yet by any means!

In fact, we could just be getting started...

Ad Aeternitatem,
The Sisters Three
(aka Sarah, Erika & Nat)

https://www.facebook.com/groups/TKGFansWrite/
https://www.facebook.com/groups/OriceranFansWrite/

OTHER TALES FROM THE KGU BOOKS

AVAILABLE AT AMAZON

Tales From the Kurtherian Universe Book One

Tales From the Kurtherian Universe Book Two

BOOKS BY MICHAEL ANDERLE

For a complete list of books by Michael Anderle, please visit

www.lmbpn.com/ma-books/

All LMBPN Audiobooks are Available at Audible.com and
iTunes. For a complete list of audiobooks visit:

www.lmbpn.com/audible

CONNECT WITH MICHAEL ANDERLE

Michael Anderle Social

Website:

http://kurtherianbooks.com/

Email List:

http://kurtherianbooks.com/email-list/

Facebook Here:

https://www.facebook.com/OriceranUniverse/

https://www.facebook.com/TheKurtherianGambitBooks/

www.ingramcontent.com/pod-product-compliance
Lightning Source LLC
Chambersburg PA
CBHW031612100726
47898CB00006B/1753